Mountain Storm

Dawn Love

Dawn Love

Photographer: FuriousFotog

Cover Model: Matthew Hosea

Cover Design: FuriousFotog

What to Know Before You Read

Mountain Storm is meant for adults and contains explicit and graphic sexual scenes and language; themes of grief, death, mental illness, PTSD, depression, violence, stalking, kidnapping, attempted murder, gun violence, and disturbing imagery. It is this author's intent to never cause harm or distress with her words. If ever you feel there should be a warning about any subject or scene in her work, please reach out to her through her social media or email so she can evaluate and consider your concerns.

https://linktr.ee/dawnlove

Stance on Generative AI

No part of this book has been knowingly created by generative AI. It is this author's stance that generative AI is detrimental to human creativity and hurts human artists and their endeavors. As such, no part of any of her work - writing, photography, narrating, cover design, editing, proofreading, illustrating, or any other service, will be knowingly crafted by generative AI. This author only uses creators she trusts to have and put forth the same values with their work. If, however, some portion of the work she has hired out is ever found to have been created by using generative AI at any time, she will do everything within her power to immediately make corrections and re-hire her work out to other service providers with the same ethical values she holds.

For those who have or are weathering their storms alone:
You are strong. You are resilient. You are needed.
You are loved.

Contents

"Be thou the rainbow in the storms of life. The evening beam that smiles the clouds away, and tints tomorrow with prophetic ray."

- Lord Byron

Chapter One

B laze pressed the button that activated the pulley system to bring the black and white target close to where he stood so he could remove the paper silhouette and take a better look at his results on the shooting grid. Pleased with what he saw, he labeled and rolled the practice paper, rubber banded it, and added it to the small pile of others on the table in front of him. Then he began the slow and methodical procedure of taking apart and cleaning the array of guns he'd used during his practice session.

Michael "Blaze" Blaisure had been coming to the practice range almost daily for the past two weeks and at least twice a week in the three and a half months before that. Yes, he wanted to keep his skills sharp, but he had a test coming up and he was determined to ace it.

He'd already been offered a deputy's position on the local police force in the quiet little town of Durbin, West Virginia, nestled at the base of the Alleghany Mountain range in Pocahontas County. Hell, he thought as he continued his clean-up, he'd pretty much been offered that position before he'd ever had the thought of becoming a cop, much less enrolling in the Police Academy.

So, for the past four months he'd made the trip to "The Hill," where he spent Monday through Friday at the Academy. He studied, he trained, and he was evaluated. He passed his background check and drug tests, and now the countdown was on. In a matter of days, he would be a Police Academy graduate - top of his class. And when he passed his final test, one given by his newly found friend, Sheriff Stephen Kaminski, he would officially be a member of the Sheriff's Department.

Over the past year and a half his life had been through more changes than he could count. He'd left the military, crashed into the side of a mountain on a cold and snowy day, and fallen into a pot of gold with the woman who had found him, unconscious and bleeding with the ass of his truck a foot off the ground and head-first in a ditch.

Through therapy and the healing love of a good woman, he'd faced some of the demons that had chased him. He had given some of them their walking papers and had been slowly learning how to deal with the rest of the fuckers.

When he left the military, the mountains had called to him, and he answered that call with the gut instinct that it was time to return to his roots. He bought property there with intentions of building a house, a home somewhere, something he could call his own for the first time in his life. But instead of building his dream home, he found his dream and his home in and with the woman he'd fallen for.

He came to the mountains to find peace, to find a place where he could be by himself and reflect on his life. He came looking for a place where he could learn to handle all those demons. Instead, he found Lexi. And when he did, the thought of living a solitary, introspective life no longer made sense. She was his peace and her love had brought a sense of healing he never thought he would achieve. She was the match to his soul. She held his heart, his joy, and his future.

Lexi Lane, the beautiful and sexy siren of the country music world. She'd made a huge splash on the Nashville music scene several years before, had become famous almost overnight, and then had disappeared in a heartbeat when tragedy struck and ripped her perfect world to pieces. She'd escaped to West Virginia and found a safe haven in the home she'd built on the top of her mountain. Within that mountain haven, she'd slowly dealt with her own demons and was, bit by bit, opening herself to the world again.

She was his everything, his angel, and he hoped it wouldn't be long until they tied the knot and made it official. To others, it might seem as if they'd moved too quickly, but to them, it had all been a natural progression. Others might think they needed to slow down, to get to know each other better, but to them, they both had found out the hard way that time has no meaning in the grand scheme of things. Sometimes, seizing the day and taking a leap into the unknown can bring about the brightest of futures and the most perfect of unions.

You could take your time in getting to know someone, plan every detail of your life with them, and then, in a matter of moments, have your entire world turned upside down and ripped apart. You could stand for freedom and justice and put your life on the line time after time only to lose the person closest to you in the blink of an eye. In a flash, your path in life might suddenly change direction, and many times when that happens, you're left reeling without a road map to guide you along the way.

No, in their minds, it was best to take leaps when they were presented because you just never knew what the next moment, the next day, or next week, might bring. It hadn't taken long for them to declare their love for each other, and when they'd done so, when they'd taken their leap, it had been together; heart to heart and soul to soul.

It hadn't been easy to leave her each week to train on the hill, only seeing her beautiful face on the weekends. In fact, the first two weeks of the academy he thought he would lose his fucking mind. After all they'd been through the prior spring, he now wanted nothing more than to just spend some carefree time with her. They needed some time without some crazy-ass people shooting at them and trying to tear them apart, some time to relax into a routine with each other.

When the opportunity to join the Sheriff's office presented itself, and he'd had a little time to think it over, he'd decided that he liked the idea, that it would not only give him some direction with his life professionally, but that it would be something he would excel at. His military background and special forces training were exactly what the Sheriff had been looking for.

When he'd pulled up the Academy website to see what it would involve and to gather logistical information, he'd seen that a new class was getting ready to start. Never one to let grass grow under his feet, he'd jumped at the opportunity, and with Lexi's full and unwavering support, had enrolled immediately.

Now, he'd finished his Academy training, and though he knew without a doubt he would pass the test the

Sheriff would give him in the morning, he wanted one more practice session. He'd always wanted to be the best, to excel at whatever was in front of him, and this test was no different. He needed to be as perfect, and as accurate as he could be, and that need was making him edgy.

Thinking of the best way to handle that edginess, he smiled mischievously. Then he gathered his guns and ammo, the results of his target practice, and made his way out to his truck. As he started the engine, his phone's Bluetooth connected, and country music came pouring from the speakers with a familiar and comforting twang. Soon he was singing along with Travis Tritt about it being a great day to be alive and daydreaming as he imagined hugging and kissing the red-headed beauty that would be waiting for him when he got home.

The bright sun glinted off the polished wood of the baby grand piano as it filtered through the leaves and branches of the tall oaks that surrounded the yard, and through the floor-to-ceiling windows that looked out upon the gorgeous view of the mountainside. The two-story A-frame cabin was large and spacious and was designed so that it appeared to grow naturally out of the land on which it was situated. The long and winding gravel driveway that invited visitors to the house was barely visible through the fullness of the tall trees and lush vegetation that grew in abundance from Spring through Fall. The land that made the backdrop for the house rose in the air behind it, a slow and steady climb from yard to mountain that quickly turned into more rugged terrain the closer you drew to the top.

And once you reached that top, the view was unhindered no matter which direction you looked. You could see vast beauty for miles and miles, and it was absolutely breathtaking.

Lexi sat at her piano playing through the melody that had been running through her mind for the past few days. Her auburn hair was piled high on top of her head in a messy bun accentuated by a Number 2 yellow pencil jutting from the base of the knot. Deep in concentration, she never noticed when first one, and then another, of her wavy curls slipped from the knot to rest against her neck.

As she played the melody she added the bass line, then gradually began building harmonies to fill out the skimpy sounding measures of music, giving it fully rounded richness the melody alone was lacking. Each time the notes reached her ears with the sound she was seeking, she pulled the pencil from her hair and scratched out the results onto line after line of staff paper.

The day had been a hot one for late August, and after only a short time outside weeding her flower beds, Lexi had sought the coolness offered by the central air conditioning unit currently keeping her home at a comfortable seventy-two degrees. The spaghetti strap tank top she wore still showed faint signs of perspiration as it clung to her curvy body. The light freckling across her shoulders had darkened throughout the summer as she'd worked outside maintaining her yard and grounds. And when she hadn't been working, her tan had been intensified by the breaks she had taken to just enjoy the peacefulness of her property, lazing completely naked in the sunshine.

In her mind, there wasn't much better, nothing quite as sumptuous, as stretching out on a blanket on the ground and letting the sun warm each and every part of your body. Connecting with the earth, the sky, and the sounds of nature always made her feel more enlightened and alive – at peace. And the look that her man had given her the first time he'd seen her after the sun had bronzed her skin and darkened her nipples, had made her heady with sensuality.

With a satisfied sigh, she played the final chord of the song she was writing and used a foot pedal to sustain the note while she quickly wrote down her most recent changes to the song. Then she went back to the beginning and started adding in the words, the lyrics that had been resonating in her soul as she'd composed, her rich alto voice filling the room with velvet tones as it echoed throughout the studio.

When she had the song just as she wanted it, she took a deep breath and stepped over to her recording equipment. She turned dials, she pressed buttons, and she adjusted levers, and then with the equipment capturing every note, she began to play and sing one more time. When the last note ended and the room was silent once more, she walked over to the equipment and stopped the recording. Then, holding her breath as she anticipated the outcome of her efforts, she hit the playback button so she could hear the results of her hard work.

There'd been a time when she thought she would never play or sing again – when even humming had been too painful. But when Blaze had come into her life, portions of herself that she thought were gone forever had returned to her bit by bit. Now, she was playing and singing better than she had before she'd left Nashville, before her fiancé and her parents had been taken from her in tragic accidents.

Concentrating on her work, she closed her eyes and let herself get lost in the sound and feel of the words and music as her song poured from the speakers once more.

Blaze closed the front door behind him and set his duffle bag down as he tugged off his heavy shit-kicker boots, tucked the laces inside, and placed them on the mat next to Lexi's sneakers. Raising his arms over his head and then backward to stretch out his back and shoulders from the lengthy drive, he made his way down the hall to Lexi's studio. When he heard her recorded voice echoing through the speakers of her sound system, he leaned against the open doorway, crossed his arms over his chest, closed his eyes, and smiled as he immersed himself in the beauty of her sound.

When the song stopped, he walked into the room and slipped his arms around her from behind, leaning forward to nuzzle her neck. "Mmm…There you are."

She leaned her head back against his shoulder. "Hey there."

He began placing kisses along the line of her neck, across her jaw, "Damn, I've missed you, Lexi!" And when she turned her head, she met his lips with her own. Passion met passion, and hands began to roam. He cupped her breasts through the thin material of her tank top and then looked down at his hands and fingers as they molded the swells, and his thumbs brushed her puckered nipples.

"That right there is a sexy sight. Watching my hands teasing you, seeing the physical confirmation of how much you want me, how much you want me to touch you, how much you want me to please you, makes me want to pound my cock into you."

"Blaze..." The breathy moan she released with his name sent sexual need straight to his cock, hardening him instantly.

"I know I just got here, but I need you, Lexi. I need to feel your heat as I pleasure you. I'll truly be home when I'm inside you, Angel."

She turned in his arms and locked her hands behind his head. Then looking up into his chocolate brown eyes she offered herself, "Take me. Fill me. I'm yours, Blaze. Welcome home..."

She jumped, wrapping her long legs around his waist and he caught her, holding tightly as he walked to the piano bench and sat down with her in his lap. He peeled her tank top off over her head and leaned forward to bury his head between her breasts. With rounded per-fection in each hand, and his thumbs teasing her nip-ples, he turned his head side to side, kissing each swell and the valley between.

Then he took a nipple in his mouth, teasing the tip to stiffness, sucking it in and releasing it with an au-dible pop of his lips before turning to her other nipple and doing the same. Her hands held his head against her breasts, caressing the baldness he preferred, and tracing his scalp. His hands moved to the waistband of her flimsy cotton shorts, then lower and when he found her wet, arousal all but pouring from her, he growled his pleasure. Then reaching between her legs with both hands, he grabbed the thin material and shredded it, exposing her panty-less pussy and all its dripping glory.

"Fuck, Lexi. I want inside you so badly, but I need a taste. I need to taste your sweetness, Angel."

She nodded her head in agreement and he picked her up and carried her around to the side of the piano where he laid her down gently. Then he pushed back her legs, exposing her fully, and once more moaned loudly, deeply, as he slowly lowered his head and drew in an arousing breath, filling his lungs with her sweet and heady aroma.

Her arousal glistened and his tastebuds tingled. He licked up one side of her pussy and then the other, slow-ly, teasing her before diving into her center. Honeyed liquid filled his mouth, and he drank from her like a man dying of thirst before working up to her clit. The taut bundle of nerves protruded from her body in excitement, and he grinned as he sucked it in.

His tongue circled in one direction before teasing her and circling back the other way. Quick flicks of the tip of his tongue that made her body tremble were quickly followed by long, slow, licks using the full width to being her pleasure. And when he felt her orgasm begin to rip through her body, he sucked once again, sending her soaring. The growl that rumbled from deep within his chest vibrated against her pussy and as the sensations overwhelmed her, her eyes rolled back in her head and she floated, lost in blissful abandon.

His cock throbbed behind his jeans, and he reached for the button, then looking up at Lexi, he saw that she'd propped herself up on her arms so she could watch him undress. Amusement lit his eyes followed immediately by lust. "Like what you see, Angel?"

"You're such a tease, Michael Blaisure!"

He began lowering his jeans and his long, rock-hard cock bobbed in anticipation. "You love every minute of it. Now," he grabbed her, easily lifting her off the piano, and she wrapped her legs around him once more, "let's tease each other." He sat back down on the piano stool and holding her by the hips, raised her until her body was perched over his cock, then he watched as her pussy lowered onto him, his shaft disappearing inside her, inch by glorious inch.

When she surrounded him, taking his breath with her tightness, he held her in place, basking in the heat that radiated from her core. Her hips tried to rock against him, but his strength won out as he relished the tightness that made his heart race as they joined together. As he savored, her hands began roaming his chest, his shoulders, and his well-defined biceps, doing one of her favorite pastimes, tracing the tattoos and scars that covered him. He liked to say he was a walking coloring book, and she whole-heartedly agreed, continually fascinated by the designs he bore on his skin.

It seemed that no matter how many times she looked at him, no matter how many times she traced each and every line, following the colors and shapes, she found something new. It wasn't only his tattoos that mesmerized her. No, this man, the man who held her heart, intoxicated her from the top of his bald head to the tip of his toes.

He finally released her and they began moving as one, their bodies coming apart and meeting time after time. When her head fell back and the breath backed up in her lungs, her inner walls began to clench around him. He stilled his body so he could experience her orgasm, so he could feel the pleasure they brought each other, but he wasn't done. No, he was a long way from having his thirst for her quenched.

He let her ride out the waves, let her catch her breath, and then he rose and walked to the edge of the room, bracing her back against the wall. Then his hips started pumping inside her once more and he set up a punishing pace.

When at last his cock began to stiffen, and the teetering edge of his impending orgasm gave way and pushed him over the cliff, he let go of the thin rope he'd been clinging to. As he let go of that rope, he grabbed onto Lexi for dear life as his cum shot out in hot jets, filling her to overflowing.

He rested his head on her shoulder and kissed her neck while his body pulsed and throbbed, buzzing with pleasure. She was his lifesaver when the seas got rough, the glowing lighthouse in his darkness, and the safe harbor that he knew would always be waiting for him.

Home. She was his home no matter where they were, and he was home at last.

Three days later Sheriff Stephen Kaminski stood with his wife Sandra, arm around her waist, as they mingled amongst the cadets and families waiting for the graduation ceremony to begin. A mixture of anticipated excitement rippled through the crowd with a healthy dose of pride and accomplishment.

"Are you ready for this, Blaze?"

"Yes, sir, Sheriff!"

"Good. I can tell you that we're certainly ready to have you on staff. Losing one of my deputies to the State Police has had us short-staffed for too long. I took this position as a retirement job, and I can tell you that I've been putting in many more hours than I had intended when I signed on. For that matter, Deputy Shaver has been too. We're both looking forward to having a regular day off again. Now," he turned to Lexi, "the better question may be, are you ready for this? Being a LEO wife can be a difficult thing to do." He tightened his hold on his wife's waist, hugging her a bit closer as he thought back over the difficult years they'd gone through together.

"Yeah, I think so." Lexi looked up at Blaze, pure love written all over her face. "I mean, I know it isn't going to be easy to be waiting at home while he's at work. I know there are going to be times that his job is a breeze and there are going to be times that his job will be extremely dangerous, but I have the utmost faith in him, his incredibly sharp mind, and his abilities. If it makes him happy, gives him some of that purpose and direction he was looking for when he left the military, then I'm behind him all the way."

Blaze hugged her close and kissed her cheek, then before they had a chance to say anything further, all the cadets were asked to take their seats so the ceremony could begin. When the time came for him to cross the stage and accept his honors, he saluted with pride. And when he looked out into the audience and met the tear-glistened, green eyes of the woman he loved, he knew that the next chapter of his life had fully begun.

Chapter Two

The aroma of bacon frying wafted through the house and woke him early on the morning of his first official day on the job. Smiling and happy because she'd made the effort to send him off on a high note, he rolled onto his back and stretched then looked down to where the thin sheet formed a perfect tent over the stiffness of his cock. He glanced quickly out the bedroom door as he wondered how receptive she would be to him walking downstairs naked and taking her on the kitchen table.

While he knew she'd be open to it, there were other things to consider. He glanced at the clock, calculated the time for sex, shower, breakfast, and the drive down the mountain. With a sigh, he decided that might be pushing it a bit. He didn't want to be late on his first day, and if he got his cock in Lexi, he might not stop for a long while. Instead, he walked into the bathroom, turned the shower on to warm up the water, and turned on some 90's hard rock to get his blood pumping.

He was almost done with his shower when he sensed her presence. With his head leaned back under the spray as the last of the soap bubbles traveled down his body in slick rivulets, he felt her hands grab onto his hips and her mouth begin to lick and tease one of his nipples, tugging gently on his barbell piercing. His cock was instantly hard again.

"Mmm...Good morning, Lexi."

She smiled against his chest as she began kissing her way down his body. "Not yet it's not..."

He opened his eyes and looked down at her as she worked her way toward his cock, taunting him as she went. When she licked the bulbous head of his hard length and then traced the thick veins that pulsed beneath his skin, his heart skipped a beat, "Oh! Well, then...by all means, let's make it a good one."

On her knees while the hot water rained down, she gently cupped his balls as she licked a droplet of pre-cum from the tip. She looked up into his warm chocolate eyes as she did, a mischievous grin tugging at the corners of her mouth. Then she began to torture him by taking him in excruciatingly slow, bit by bit. Her tongue teased and taunted as she sucked him down as far as she could, then she opened her throat and slid to the base. He gasped and groaned in ecstasy.

She held there as long as she could before coming up for air, her gag reflex tripping lightly. And when she did, she grinned up at him once more and repeated her pleasureful play. Again her tongue traced the veins of his cock as his blood pounded beneath the surface, pulsing and throbbing in time with his rapid heartbeats. When she took him in again, she began to set up a rhythm, sucking back up his shaft and immediately going back down the full length of his cock.

It didn't take long for him to reach the pinnacle of pleasure. When he did, one palm slammed the wall of the shower to try to steady himself while the other hand tangled in her wet hair. He tugged gently at the roots of her hair as he held her in place and plunged his cock as deep as it would go, and with her lips suctioned around him, he came, filling her mouth with hot streams of cum.

He released her, and when he did, she looked up at him with a teasing light in her eyes. She swallowed and continued sucking, licking all the cum from his cock and making his knees weak.

"Oh, God! No. No more! I can't take it, babe!" The agonized chuckle that escaped him had him feeling and sounding slightly insane. She released his cock with a giggle and kissed the tip. Then he joined her on the floor of the shower and pulled her into his lap, hugging her tightly to him.

"Now, it's a good morning."

"Lexi. Every morning with you is a good morning. This just makes it better."

"I made you breakfast."

"Mmh hmm, I smell bacon and coffee, and I think I smell something sweet."

"Cinnamon rolls."

"Oh, I smelled that, too, but I was talking about this." With one long finger, he pushed inside her pussy, her overflowing arousal allowing him to slide in easily. He pulled out and then slid in two fingers, working her, working her g-spot. When he pulled his fingers out once more, he placed them against his lips and looking her in the eye, licked her from his fingers.

"Yeah, that's the sweetness I smelled. So tasty! I need more of that!"

The sexy laugh that escaped her made his heart flipflop with happiness and contentment. "Well, that sounds amazing, but if we do that, you're going to be late. You know that you can never stop with one orgasm."

"True. Very true. Raincheck for tonight when you're hard-working man gets home from the trenches?"

"Oh, definitely! I'll be ready and waiting for you to have your wicked way with me, Deputy."

"Perfect!"

Lexi leaned against the frame of the open front door and with a contented smile on her face and a half-finished cup of coffee in hand, watched as Blaze's truck disappeared down the driveway. She shook her head as she thought of how truly rotten he was.

He actually let her believe that he would let her pleasure him and hold off until he returned home from work to return the favor to her. But as she'd stood up to leave the shower, he'd grabbed her, turned her to him, and had his mouth on her in an instant. The move had been lightning fast and she hadn't seen it coming.

The combination of the move, his mouth and tongue, and the arousal that had already been coursing through her body had made her orgasm immediately. And while he'd complained about not having time for more, he'd made it perfectly clear that he'd never let her pleasure him and then walk away without receiving her own.

She didn't think he could be more amazing or that she could love him more.

She stepped back into the house and hurried to the kitchen to clean up from breakfast. She'd already seen to the animals, the goats and chickens she kept for milk and eggs, and once the kitchen was set to rights, she had to get herself ready for a long day of meetings. Granted, they were virtual, so that would help matters along, but the plans she'd been making on the sly would be getting more concrete in their undertaking today and she wanted to be on top of her game.

While Blaze had been away over the summer, she'd been writing again, composing, recording, and she now had a full dozen songs she was sending to the head of the record label in Nashville where she'd previously signed. She couldn't wait to get his feedback.

She sighed as she thought of that time in her life – her time in Nashville before her world had crumbled around her. Night after night performing at local bars and praying that she'd catch the eye of the head of some music label. And when those prayers were answered and her dreams began to come true, she'd celebrated with her now deceased lover. She'd been happy, or so she'd thought, but so naive. She'd been young and in love with being in love. Not that she hadn't loved Jackson, her childhood sweetheart, teenage boyfriend, and fiancé, but looking back she now realized that it had been the blush of first love and the ideals of love itself that had clouded her heart and mind.

After meeting Blaze and discovering true love and all that it entailed, she could see just how wrong she and Jackson had been for each other. She often wondered what would have happened if he hadn't died in the murky waters of the Cumberland River. Would they have been happy? Would their relationship have survived? Looking back on it without the rose-tinted glasses and her eyes fully open, she truly didn't think so. Some things are meant to be and some simply aren't.

Glancing at the clock on the stove she realized she'd gotten lost in her musings and was now pressed for time. She emptied the dishwater from the sink and hung her drying towel on the dishrack before hurrying upstairs to take a quick shower and dress for the day.

Blaze wasn't sure what he'd expected but walking into the station and being greeted with a "Welcome!" banner and the Sheriff's elderly assistant holding out a steaming mug of coffee hadn't been it. Nor had he expected the small group assembled below the sign. The station didn't have many employees, but they were all there, including Sheriff Kaminski who was finishing a phone call. Deputy Shaver was there as well, and shook his hand as he offered a gruff welcome, then quickly disappeared into the back of the building. He accepted the coffee, thanking Ms. Eliza as he did, and looked up to see the Sheriff had risen from his desk and was headed his way.

"Deputy."

"Sheriff." Blaze took a sip of the coffee and found that she'd doctored it just the way he liked – two sugars and a splash of cream. He stared at the cup in confusion.

"Son, I don't know how she does it, she just does. I don't ask and she doesn't tell. Actually, that's the way it is with most administrative things around here. She just makes it happen. It's like magic how things just appear before they're even needed and get done before anyone asks. I never have to tell her when things need doing, it just happens. I don't know what we'll do when she finally decides she's had enough of babysitting our asses and retires."

"Well, then, I suppose I'll have to make extra effort to stay on Ms. Eliza's good side."

"You can say that again. Come on back to my desk and let's get some of this hiring paperwork out of the way so we can get down to the good stuff."

"Lead the way, Sheriff."

When the paperwork was complete and dutifully handed to Ms. Eliza for processing, the Sheriff briefed Blaze on their pending cases.

"Two drunk and disorderly, one domestic violence, and some teens joyriding? That's it?"

"Yeah. Like I told you, for the most part, it's a fairly quiet job in a quiet area. It's what attracted me to the position when I left the NYPD. In fact, everything that happened to you and Lexi in the spring was the biggest and most involved case I've handled since I started here as Sheriff."

Blaze thought back to the nightmare that he and Lexi had lived through. Being shot at, stalked, and an attempted kidnapping by a man and woman who were clearly not in their right minds had brought him some of the scariest moments of his life.

The image of Melinda Osborne as she'd gone after Lexi, the crazed look in her eyes, and the moment his heart had stopped as he'd realized that Lexi had decided to take matters into her own hands, flashed through his mind in quick succession. When she'd reached for her iron skillet and used it like a baseball bat against Melinda's head, his lungs had clenched, and he hadn't been able to breathe. It hadn't been until he'd seen Melinda's body crumpled and unresponsive on the floor that he'd felt his heart begin to beat again and his lungs fill with air.

"I try hard not to think about that time, at least as far as anything directly related to David and Melinda Osborne."

"I can understand that, and I can tell you that I've tried to put it out of my mind as much as I possibly can, as well. But I don't think I'll ever forget being held at gunpoint and then hearing the unmistakable echo of a shot fired. I'm very thankful that your friend has such amazing aim. If not, I might not be here to welcome you on your first day."

Blaze nodded his head in agreement as he thought back to the information that had been relayed to him and Lexi as Melinda had been rolled out of the house on a gurney, still unconscious from the hard hit that Lexi had given. While they'd been dealing with Melinda, the Sheriff and one of Blaze's military buddies had been at the Osborne house gathering evidence.

They'd thought that David had been the mastermind behind all the trouble that kept showing up on Blaze and Lexi's doorstep, but it had turned out that David and Melinda both had been up to their eyeballs in the mess. So, while the Sheriff had gone to the Osborne house to talk to Melinda, it had actually been David that he'd had a run-in with. And though the sheriff had tried to talk to him, to reason with him, it had only taken a few moments to determine that David had lost all capability of rational thinking.

He'd pulled his gun and aimed it at the sheriff as the sheriff had stood on the porch in disbelief over the sad and gruesome scene that he'd found in the Osborne house. When he'd gone to pull the trigger, Blaze's friend who had been carefully searching the property for bombs and traps, had fired first. Fearing for the sheriff's life, he'd taken David out with a single shot right between the eyes. It had been an intense and scary situation, no matter which way you looked at it.

"How about we go and have a talk with some parents? Maybe we can put some fear in a few teenagers and keep 'em from causing an accident in the future." The Sheriff smiled mischievously. "I reckon that when they get a look at my new deputy it might cause these boys to think twice about getting out of line again."

Blaze grinned as he followed the sheriff out the door and climbed into the passenger seat of his truck. The threat of legal consequences delivered by an intimidating man with bulging muscles, deep scars, and skin tattooed with a colorful array of graffiti, would probably work like magic for delivering their message.

The spicy aroma of Italian herbs and spices scented the air as the lasagna Lexi made earlier in the day warmed in the oven. Music filled the once silent rooms – an added detail that she'd not been able to enjoy for many years before Blaze had come into her life. The darkness of the house was relieved only by dimmed lights and the glowing flames of tall, white taper candles she'd placed on the kitchen table. The plates and flatware gleamed in the soft candlelight, and a bottle of red wine sat uncorked on the table to breathe.

Lexi had pulled her hair off her neck once again and had loosened tendrils of her auburn locks from the French twist to lay perfectly against her cheeks and the nape of her neck. Gold glinted at her ears, at her wrist, and the gentle lighting in the room shimmered across the material of the emerald-green wrap dress she'd chosen specifically for this occasion.

When she heard Blaze's truck coming up the driveway, she hurried to the door, excited anticipation coursing through her, and waited to greet him with a mischievous smile. She watched as he climbed the stairs of the wide front deck and stood staring at her, arms behind his back, with a devilish grin of his own.

"Welcome home."

"My God you do know how to paint a picture, Lexi. You take my breath away, Angel."

She held out a hand to him to draw him inside, but when he didn't immediately take it, she gave him a quizzical look. "Is something wrong?"

"No. Everything is perfect. I do have a surprise, though, and even though I think you'll love it, I'm sort of second-guessing myself right now."

"What? What is it? Come on. You know I'll love whatever it is because it came from you."

At that moment she heard a soft whimper and the sound of a small nose snuffling. Lexi's eyes widened in wonder.

"Blaze. What have you done?"

With a soft chuckle, he brought his hands from behind his back and up to his chest to cradle the tiny brown bundle that wriggled and squirmed with happiness. Lexi gasped in surprise.

"Oh, a puppy! You brought me a puppy?!" She reached for the dark ball of fur with a smile that stretched from ear to ear and brought a twinkle to her eyes. When she tucked the puppy close to her chest, she began to murmur soft words of love and kissed it on the head.

Blaze released the breath he hadn't been aware he was holding. He hadn't been certain what her reaction to the puppy would be, but he thought, had hoped, she would be pleased. Seeing the instant love between the two of them relieved his mind.

"Well, there's a story there." They stepped inside and made their way over to the sofa. They sat with the puppy between them, and Blaze began telling her about his day as Lexi rubbed and scratched on the puppy.

"So, there we were talking to this kid's parents and I'm hearing all this barking and whining coming from the back of the house. I asked about the dog and the kid went and opened the gate to try to calm it down. Next thing I know, here comes the momma. She sniffs me over, sniffs over the sheriff, and then she takes off to the back of the house again. I figured well, she's decided we're alright, because she'd calmed right down after she checked us out. A couple of minutes later she came trotting out of the back with this little guy in her mouth, plops her butt down in front of me and looks up at me with these big, sweet eyes, and places the puppy in my lap.

"I was shocked and a little bit confused, but the momma laid her head on my lap, and I swear when she looked up at me it was almost as if she was smiling. I'm not quite sure how it happened, but the kid's parents insisted that I take the pup, and somehow or another I walked out of there with him. Sheriff K had warned me that the people around here tend to push food, firewood, or whatever they have on hand at you when you go to calls, but I can't say that I would have expected someone to give me a dog. Crazy, huh?"

"Extremely! But, oh, he's so sweet!"

"We haven't talked about getting a pet."

"No. We haven't. And while I can't say I had given it any thought, I'm certainly not against it."

"Good. I got to thinking about it after we left, when I was still unsure what to do with him, and decided that I really liked the idea of us having a dog around. Not only will he be good company when I'm at work, but if we train him, he might be an extra layer of protection."

Lexi looked up at him for the first time since he'd started telling her the puppy's story and saw a glimmer of the worry that he always tried so hard to hide. She knew there were times that he still thought about the danger they'd faced in the spring, that he worried, even though the danger was long gone.

"Blaze."

"Lexi, I know you can handle yourself. You're quite the badass with a frying pan and you know how to handle a gun, but you're not going to stop me from worrying. I love you and part of me loving you is worrying about your safety. If we keep him, train him, it will help ease my mind some."

"I know." She hugged the puppy close and buried her face in his fluffy fur once more. "You don't have to convince me; I'm already in love with him. Trained for protection or not, he's ours. What breed is he? Do you know?"

"He's an Akita Shepherd. They bred a male German Shepherd with a female Akita. I did some research when we got back to the office and the mixture should mean that he will be extremely smart, loyal, and protective. He should be everything we could possibly want in a dog."

"Oh! We're going to need puppy stuff and food, and, oh my goodness!" She picked up her fluffy bundle and turned him so that she could look him in the face. "Well...you're going to need a name, aren't you, cutie?"

Blaze chuckled as he watched Lexi fall head over heels for the pup. "You name him whatever you want. He's sure going to be one lucky little guy getting you for a dog mom."

Lexi gasped, "That's it! Lucky. We'll call him Lucky!"

Reaching for the puppy, Blaze grinned as he studied his face and examined his furry features, "Is that your name? Lucky? Yeah, I think Lucky works just fine." The puppy wiggled excitedly, and he hugged him close only to have four paws begin to try to climb his chest, licking Blaze on the chin and cheek to share his happiness.

"I did stop and grab a bag of puppy food, but we'll need to pick out some chew toys, a leash, maybe even a crate. I thought you might want a hand in picking out those things."

"Absolutely!"

"Now," he grinned as he looked her up and down, "something is making my mouth water."

"Lasagna. It does smell good, doesn't it?"

"Well, that's making my mouth water, too, but I was talking about you." He took his time as he studied her inch by inch, admiring the sexy image she made in the dress she'd chosen.

Lexi's bell-like laughter sent shivers down his spine. He put the puppy down on the carpet so he could explore his new home and then held out a hand to Lexi, pulling her to him and into his lap. When she was settled across his thick, muscular thighs, he crushed her lips with his own.

He caressed her face and loosened the bun atop her head. When her hair was freed, he ran his hands through the lush mass of red curls as he continued to claim her mouth. He took his time as he tasted, teased, and enjoyed the feel of her body as her muscles began to slowly melt and turn into a puddle beneath his touch.

He drew the kiss out until they were breathless. As they finally came up for air, he kissed her softly, once, twice, three times, before placing his forehead against hers and soaking up the perfection of the moment as they reconnected after their long day apart.

"I missed you today, Lexi."

"I missed you, too. How about we eat, and you can finish telling me about your day, and then I can tell you about mine?"

"Sounds perfect!"

Chapter Three

"So, there we were, finishing our lunches over at Ma's diner and in runs this kid, maybe eleven or twelve years old and he's yelling for someone to come quick, that Old Man Jeffries and Mr. Handy have gotten into an argument over their daily game of checkers and that they're yelling and threatening each other.

"Evidently, the last time this happened they caused property damage. One of them slashed the other's truck tires, and the other retaliated by stealing some of the coils to his homemade moonshine still." Blazed chuckled as he relayed the story.

"We managed to break it up and they called a truce, but I don't think that's the last I'll be hearing from them. I guess it is a long-standing tradition for them to be the best of friends one minute, then go at each other the next when things don't go like they want."

"They sound like quite the pair!"

"Yeah, other than that it was a pretty quiet day."

"Well, I have something I want to talk to you about."

"Alright, go for it."

Lexi took a deep breath, "You know I've been writing, composing, recording." She scooped up a bite of lasagna and chewed slowly while she gathered her courage to continue. "I got in touch with my old record label and sent them the demos I'd put together. Blaze...they loved them!"

"Oh my God, Lexi! That's fantastic! And of course, they loved them! What's not to love?"

"I was just so unsure about jumping back into the music scene, getting involved with all of that again."

"So, what are you thinking here? An album? A tour?"

"Whoa. Not so fast." Lexi laughed at his enthusiasm.

"Alright. I've told you repeatedly that I'll support you, no matter what."

"I know. And I think, for now, at least, I'm content with the writing, the composing. It gives me the chance to do what I love, be a part of what I enjoy, without completely losing myself in the business.

"Okay. Yeah. I can see that."

"The record company wants all of the songs, Blaze. Each and every one of them. I've got my attorney hammering out the final details, but I should have royalty streams for years to come off of these songs."

"Lexi. I'm so damn proud of you." Blaze took her hand and held it between both of his, tenderly caressing the back. "I know how hard it was for you to step back into your studio, to reach deep inside yourself and unlock that door. Watching you as you've found that part of yourself again, as you've opened yourself to the music inside you again, has been such an amazing experience. There's this glow radiating from you now and it just gets brighter with each passing day."

"I guess we've both come a long way in a short period of time."

"Yeah. We have."

Lexi dabbed at the corner of her eye, wiping absently at an unshed tear. "Whew. Okay. There's more."

Blaze, finished with his meal, sat back in his chair and stretched his legs out in front of him, crossing them at the ankles and relaxing his body as he waited for her to continue.

"I have an idea for what to do with the property you bought."

The acreage, originally intended to be the site of Blaze's dream home, sat approximately fifteen miles away from their cabin. When he and Lexi had fallen in love and he moved into the home she'd built, he'd put his plans for the property aside until he could figure out exactly what they wanted to do with it. They talked about selling it. They talked about leaving it as it was, wooded and natural. They'd even talked about building a second home on it to rent out, but no matter how many ideas they came up with, they hadn't hit on what they really wanted.

"And what has that incredibly intelligent and sexy mind of yours come up with?"

"Whew. Umm, okay. This may sound a little crazy but let me get it all out before you point out the flaws. Picture this: a summer camp for aspiring musicians — teenagers - middle and high school age. There would be a main building that would house practice areas, music rooms filled with a huge array of instruments. Another building would hold the dining hall and kitchen. There would be cabins for the campers and counselors, and, of course, a small amphitheater where there would be performances, maybe even an indoor stage in case of bad weather.

"It would only be open during the summer, of course, and we would concentrate on whatever area the campers wanted to learn about or improve upon. I could hire instructors for voice, for piano, for wood-winds and brass, for percussion — maybe even someone who could work with them on composition.

"I would be able to do what I love and in turn, I could give back by sharing, teaching, and molding future generations of musicians. And, as the property is close, if I needed to step back – for whatever reason – I would still be able to keep an eye on things.

Lexi chuckled nervously. "And now that I've said all that out loud it definitely sounds insane."

"Lexi." Blaze stood up and walked around the table before holding his hand out to her. She placed her hand in his calloused palm and he pulled her to her feet before hugging her closely. "I think that is a brilliant idea."

"You do?"

"Yeah, I do."

"Okay. Can you tell me exactly why you think it is a brilliant idea? Because I'm seriously second-guessing myself here."

"Alright. One," he pulled back far enough so he could look into the vivid green of her eyes, "you've been wanting an outlet for your music – this accomplishes that. Two, having your name associated with a music camp would be a big draw. Three, not only is it a way for you to make music, be involved with music, and share your music, but it is an excellent and extremely smart business venture.

"Four, it would only be open during a few months of the year so it wouldn't be something that you would have to do full time, which allows you breathing room for working on your own music. Five, it gives us a use for that property, and it is an amazing spot for something like that.

"I love the idea, Angel."

"Really?"

"Yeah. Really."

"You don't think it's too weird combining music with an actual camp? I mean, I've heard of music camps, but they're usually done someplace like a college campus or at a musical theater."

"I absolutely don't think it's weird. Tell me this – why do you want to combine music and nature?"

"Oh, wow. Okay. There's music all around us. You can hear it everywhere. But there's just something about being up here in the mountains, hearing nature's music – whether that's birds singing or crickets chirping, or something as simple as the sound that a breeze makes as it ruffles the leaves on the trees. It clears your mind and opens you to other sounds you might not always pay attention to. Nature's music is such a beautiful song.

"I remember all those nights that my family spent camping at the lakes in Kentucky and falling asleep to the trill of a Screech Owl or the call of a Whippoorwill, the soft lapping of the lake water as it met the shore. And, there's more, so much more!

"Being out in nature brings me such clarity, opens my mind and inspires me. You know how much I love the outdoors and just being one with nature. When we started thinking about all those acres and what we might do with them, we said we wanted to do something that would make an impact but would also respect the land. We wanted something that would not only make a difference, for me, for us, and for future generations, but something that we could possibly make a profit on, and everything just fell into place. Does that make sense?"

"That right there. That look on your face. That's confirmation for me that this is exactly right. You talk about this camp and this light you have inside you just burns brighter. It will be perfect, just like you. So, what do we do first?"

Lexi laughed and she shook her head. "I should have known you would be on board with this."

"Absolutely."

"Well, I did have a meeting with my attorney today – mostly because of the song deals, but I spoke with him about what to do, how to handle this, first steps, etc., if you were in agreement. I have the architect that I used for the design of this house who would be great for drawing up plans for us. We'll need a builder, someone for the electric, septic, and water, umm, wow. There will be advertising and we'll need a web page and I'll have to hire people to run it. There will be quite a bit to do, but I really think it will work."

"What else?"

"Well, there's a decent amount of acreage there, but to make this happen we're going to have to try to buy up some of the surrounding land. I don't want everything to feel too crammed together. It will take some finessing, but I think, with all my considerable charm," she winked at him, "that I might be able to convince the property owners around us to each sell off small portions so that we can enlarge and make room for everything. And I want to make sure it's inclusive, so I definitely want to make it as handicap accessible as possible. Wow! There's just so much to consider, but I think it could be amazing!

"It will be, Angel. It'll be just as amazing as you are. Let's do it!"

Lexi took a deep breath and shook her head as she beamed at him, "Really? Let's do it? Just like that?"

"Yep! Just like that. Now, I'm going to take the puppy out and we'll see if we can get him settled for the night. Then, if I remember correctly from this morning, I have some very naughty things that I promised to do to you tonight."

He kissed her softly, tenderly, then pulled back and grinned at her before hungrily going back for more. Her lips parted as his tongue began to seek, to devour, and when he pulled away her breathing was ragged and her heartbeat erratic. He gave her a quick smack on the ass

before turning and leaving her standing there in a daze
as he whistled and called for the puppy.

Blaze stood on the back deck as the late summer sun
began to fade to dusk and watched as the energetic ball
of fur ambled about the yard, exploring as he sniffed
and peed on everything in sight. It still amazed him
sometimes that his life had changed so drastically in
such a short period of time.

In a matter of a few months, he'd gone from being
part of a top-secret military unit and traveling all over
the world, to giving it all up and wandering aimlessly
for direction, to finding an all-consuming love with the
woman of his dreams, and a new purpose and outlook
on life through a strange twist of fate.

He'd asked Lexi to be his wife in the spring, and she'd
happily agreed. They hadn't made it official, though,
and afterward, he'd quickly been immersed in studying
and training at the academy. He'd wanted to get her a
ring, to get down on his knee and be traditional with
a proposal, but it had only been in the past couple of

weeks that he'd found the time to go and hunt down the ring he'd envisioned her wearing.

He'd seen her jewelry box and knew that she kept the ring that Jackson had given her years ago. It sat in the top tray, wedged between blue velvet pillowing – a treasured but sad reminder of days past and all she'd lost.

Blaze had wanted something different, and for more than one reason. The ring he'd chosen was perfect, and he couldn't wait any longer to give it to her. Tonight, he thought, when so many new and amazing things were happening for them. Yes, tonight he was going to make it official and take them to the next step in their relationship.

With excited anticipation for what her reaction might be to the ring and their future together, he gathered the puppy and carried him inside.

With dinner cleaned up and her kitchen set to rights, Lexi went upstairs to anxiously wait for Blaze to join her. She walked into their bedroom and straight to the closet. Since Blaze had come into her life, she'd been updating and adding to her lingerie wardrobe, and she'd been hanging onto a couple of pieces for just the right moment.

Tonight, was one of those moments, she thought, and their celebration of his job, her news, and their decision about the camp deserved as many special touches as possible. As she reached for the silky material she'd hidden in the back of the closet a few weeks earlier, a chill of anticipation shimmered its way up her spine. She quickly changed and then lit candles scattered around the room. Then she turned off the lights and stretched out across the bed so she faced the doorway.

When she heard him climbing the stairs, her heart began to beat rapidly, and her body began to hum with want and need. And when he stepped into view, his large frame filling the doorway, her desire for him stirred deep in her core.

Blaze stepped into the room and seeing her lying across the bed as she waited for him, stopped in his tracks. He'd been expecting her to be waiting for him, but he didn't anticipate the soft candlelight, nor the apricot-colored satin that draped along her curves, accentuating the perfection of her body. As her tanned skin glowed in the soft light, and her smile radiated across the room toward him, he felt his heart begin to race and butterflies begin to flutter in his stomach.

Knowing without a doubt that this was it, this was the moment he'd been waiting for, he dropped to one knee and held out his hand to her. Her name floated along the silence that filled the room as it fell breathily from his lips, an answer to her siren's call.

"Lexi."

Grinning at his reaction, she rose and went to him. As she crossed the plush carpet, the satin of her gown skimmed her curves. And with every movement, her lush body was highlighted, a silhouetted flame that warmly glowed as she went to him. Unaware of his intentions, she smiled down at him as she placed her hand in his, his calloused palm a roughened contrast to the satiny smoothness of her skin.

"You take my breath away, Angel."

"Michael..."

He cut her off as he flashed his crooked grin at her. "Now, just hold on. I'm trying to do something here." She softly bit her lip as she smiled and waited for him to continue.

"I told you once that I'd been through the dark, but that you were my light. I told you that I'd lived in chaos, but that when I found you, you calmed my turmoil. I shared with you that through the years I'd crawled on my hands and knees and lost my way, but with you, I found my direction and I could finally stand tall and proud again.

"I spoke with you about my lost ideals, about the changes in me that made me unrecognizable, confused, and uncertain about who I was – uncertain of my personal truth. And I told you that with you, I'd finally found my authenticity. I found it on a freezing cold and snowy night when I opened my eyes and saw you standing before me glowing like the angel you are. My angel.

"I don't think I could be more in love with you than I am at this moment. But, then again, I thought that yesterday, and the day before that. And I've proven myself wrong time after time because I love you more and more with each passing day." Tears glistened in her eyes and though she knew what was coming, her body began to tremble with anticipation.

"Lexi. A few months ago, I asked you to marry me, and you accepted," he reached in his pocket, "but I wasn't as prepared as I should have been because I didn't have a ring, a symbol of my commitment to you, to us, and our future.

"Now," he pulled out the sparkling ring and held it at the tip of her finger as his gaze bore deeply into her eyes, "I do. This stone, an oval ruby, symbolizes love, desire, and passion. The small heart-shaped diamonds surrounding the ruby are for eternal love and devotion. And the band, three strands of interwoven white gold, represents our past, our present, and our future.

"And now, I'll ask you again. Lexi Lane, will you marry me? Will you share your life with me? Will you build on the life that we've started together and share a future with me?"

The tears that she'd held back began to track slowly down her cheeks, and she nodded her head in agreement. "Yes. Yes! I'll marry you, Blaze. Nothing would make me happier than to be your wife."

He slid the ring on her finger and pressed his lips to her knuckles before rising and gathering her close. He claimed her mouth in a sensual kiss and scooped her into his arms to carry her to the bed.

Together they stretched out across the satiny sheets and began to explore, slowly removing each other's clothes as they went. Lips kissed, tongues tasted, fingers roamed. Time stood still as they tempted and teased. And when at last he entered her, he held motionless inside her while he looked into the depths of her emerald eyes. Skin to skin they lay together - united, heart, mind, body, and soul until he could take it no longer.

When he began to move, she met his thrusts with those of her own. Their bodies collided in a dance as old as time as their need to share their love with each other consumed from within. They burned with need. They ached for release. And with each powerful stroke, they raced to completion, climbing higher and higher until their bodies took flight, soaring with all-consuming bliss.

Chapter Four

April – Two Years Later

A   Bundled against the chill of the harsh, early spring wind, Lexi stood on the rise overlooking the camp property and watched as laborers began to lay the foundation for the final building to be erected. Plans had been drawn up and approval for the camp and construction had been pushed through Planning and Zoning quickly. Red tape, it seemed, unraveled quickly when enough money was thrown at it.

The other buildings weren't complete, but even though there was still quite a bit of work to be done on the inside, the fact that the buildings were in place with a roof over them eased her mind greatly. Inside work could be done no matter the weather, but if they'd received another snowfall or heavy rain, they could have been delayed for weeks on end. She considered herself fortunate the weather had decided to be gentle the past few months.

With the weather forecast leaning toward warming temperatures and clear skies, Lexi felt certain they would remain on schedule and be ready for their first year of summer camp at Allegheny Mountain Academy of Music. Everything, it seemed, was falling into place.

With all the legalities now out of the way, she'd begun to interview for counselors and staff, and had even hired a few people that she'd immediately felt were a perfect fit. Yes, she thought, it's all coming together.

Even things in her and Blaze's personal life were starting to gel. After their whirlwind courtship and getting engaged, they decided to hold the status quo for a bit before thinking about setting a date. Waiting until the camp was up and running before they tackled the next step in their lives had been logical in their minds. Now, they were finally beginning to discuss dates and venues. It wouldn't be long, she thought, before she and Blaze made things official.

A series of barks got her attention, and she smiled as she glanced over to see Lucky bounding her direction. Though he'd grown and was now topping out at eighty-five pounds, there was still enough puppy in him that he constantly wanted to play. He circled her once then sat and dropped the stick he carried in his mouth at her feet before looking at her with a hopeful gleam in his eyes.

"Again?" She scratched his head as she reached for the stick. "Alright, but last time, okay? We have to get home so I can get some work done." With a long-practiced arm, she threw the stick as far as she could and sent the dog racing after it. He ran as hard as he could and after securing his prize in his mouth once more, began his return trip.

Before he could get back to her side, Lexi heard the unmistakable sound of an engine climbing the steep incline of the gravel driveway that had been placed so the work trucks could safely reach the campsite. Eventually, she thought, that would be replaced with something more substantial, but for the time being, it worked well enough.

As the truck came into view, Lexi called the dog to her side and gave the command to sit and stay. She watched as the driver's door opened and Bradley Hayden, the newest site foreman, stepped out to greet her. Even though he'd been working with the crew for a while, he'd only been the foreman for a couple of weeks, having taken over when the original foreman had retired and moved to South Carolina. So far, the few interactions they'd had led Lexi to firmly believe he knew what he was doing.

"Afternoon, Ms. Lane." He looked down at Lucky and smiled, "Hey there big guy!" He held out his hand and Lucky went to him, sniffing and eventually accepting the head scratches the man offered.

"Good afternoon."

"That's the last of it," he nodded toward the cement truck currently pouring the gray mixture into the foundation form. "The forecast says the weather is going to hold so in four, maybe five days, the concrete will be set and we'll be able to start framing it up. I've got three-man crews in each of the main buildings doing the punchout work. Interior walls are going up and trimming out is starting in the others. Electrical and plumbing work is coming along. The cabins are a bit easier with the most labor-intensive part being the bathrooms. Best I can tell at this point we should be finishing up right on schedule for your opening."

Lexi breathed a sigh of relief. "That's just what I was hoping to hear, Mr. Hayden. It certainly eases my mind and gives me more information to have available when I do some interviewing this afternoon."

"I hope you don't mind me asking, but how exactly did you come up with this idea for the camp?"

Lexi chuckled. "Well, the easiest explanation is that it came to me in a dream. Once the idea was planted, it just took off. Blaze and I are excited to get the camp up and running."

"Blaze?"

"Yes," she smiled up at him. "My fiance."

He grimaced before he spoke again. "I suppose that answers my next question. I should have guessed that a beautiful woman like you had someone. Just my luck," he chuckled and she smiled appreciatively at him. "Well, then I better head on down there and check things over. Good talkin' to ya, Ms. Lane. I'll keep in touch about the progress."

"Thank you. I appreciate it and all the hard work the crew has put in."

With a nod of his head, he jumped back into his truck and drove down to the site. She watched as he parked his truck in the makeshift parking area and climbed out to begin his day. Eventually, that parking area would be paved to make it more accessible for everyone working or visiting the camp. Yes, she thought, there was still quite a bit of work to do, but things were definitely progressing.

Lexi looked down to where the dog sat patiently at her feet waiting for her instruction and smiled. "Come on, Lucky. Let's go home. We have work to do for the camp and a fun little side project that I want to take care of today." With a yip and a happily wagging tail, he jumped up into the cab of the truck and Lexi climbed in after him. With one last glance around the property, she turned the truck around and began the half-hour trip back to her haven.

It had been a long day and Blaze was tired. A tourist passing through their small town hadn't been paying attention as he'd been driving through Main Street and had run a stop light – the only traffic light in the dang town – and had crashed into Ms. Eliza's car as she'd been returning from her post office run for the day. By the time he'd gotten their statements and helped them with reports for insurance and a tow truck for Ms. Eliza, he'd managed to miss lunch.

He'd placed a takeout order and was on his way to pick it up when he'd gotten the call that Old Man Jeffries and Mr. Handy had gotten into it again. This time they argued over who had gotten the bigger piece of cake over at Ma's Diner. He shook his head and rolled his eyes. Who would have thought that two men in their seventies could cause such a ruckus? And wasn't it funny that everyone called Mr. Jeffries "Old Man" when he and Mr. Handy were the same age? The argument had been epic. Cups and plates had been broken, and their poor waitress had ended up with chocolate cake and icing smashed into her hair when the generous slices of cake went flying across the diner.

At least, he thought, he'd already been heading in the direction of the diner when the fight broke out. It had taken every negotiating skill he had and the threat of a few hours in a cell to calm the men. But after paying for the damages and helping to clean up their mess, they'd walked out of the diner the best of friends once again.

Blaze had grabbed his takeout order at that point and had hurried back to the station, only to be met with yet another call. This one had taken him out of town and up into the mountains where a toddler had wandered away from his home while his exhausted mother had napped on the couch. He'd taken charge of the situation and quickly formed a search team. Although the little tyke had gone a good distance, they'd found him quickly and returned him to his worried mama. Joyful tears had fallen as the mama hugged her toddler closely and repeatedly thanked the team for their assistance.

He'd missed dinner time with Lexi and had ended up once again grabbing food on the go. By the time he had started up the mountain toward home, it was getting late. It was rare that he had to work past normal shift times, but sometimes it was just unavoidable.

Now, as he parked his truck and glanced up at the gleaming lights of home, he exhaled a sigh of relief and tried his best to put the worries of the day behind him. Tomorrow, after all, would be arriving quickly and he hated to waste a single moment on things that were over and done when he could be spending that time with Lexi.

When he walked in the door he found Lucky sitting and waiting for him, tail wagging once more, with a note attached to his collar. He grinned when he opened it and read the message out loud.

Aladdin's cave is full of treasures but none can compare. A trove of delights awaits upstairs. Don't hesitate; don't be late. I won't start without you, but please don't make me wait, for the needs I have, only you can sate. You shared your dream and I've made it a reality. Welcome home, my love. Hurry now and come to me.

His heart beat out of time, thudding hard in his chest as he read her note once more and stared in disbelief. Months and months ago he'd told her of a dream he'd had where they'd turned their spare bedroom into a sexual playroom paradise. He'd woken from that dream with Lexi's lips around his cock and her dripping pussy in his face. When he'd finally recovered from the pleasures they'd given and found with each other, he'd described the dream to her in explicit detail. They'd laughed and joked about his kinky side, and he'd thought that had been the end of the discussion.

Was it possible, he wondered, that she'd decided to fulfill some of his fantasies? Never one to hesitate when there was something he wanted, he quickly ran up the stairs to find out. With his hand wrapped around the doorknob, he paused long enough to try to calm himself as anticipation surged throughout his body, electric energy zinging through his nerve endings. Then turning the knob and swinging the door open wide, he blinked in disbelief. The sight that met him was almost an exact replica of what he'd dreamed.

The bed where they'd first made love had been replaced, and the metal framing of the new bed was outfitted with restraints. The red satin sheets she'd chosen added a vibrant and sensual contrast to the dark frame. A Saint Andrews cross was the focal point of one wall - the black iron cross accentuated with red padding at the wrists, ankles, and lower back while black cuffs waited to secure one's extremities. A spanking bench sat in one corner, and a portable sex swing sat in another. A black leather flip-top storage bench sat with the top open and though he only had an obstructed view from the doorway of the room, he could tell she'd loaded it with sex toys.

As for Lexi, she waited for him in a skimpy black leather bondage suit. The top of the suit, a bra with cutouts that left her rounded and perky breasts bare. The bottom, a low-waisted panty with an open slit that ran from front to back. Each piece of the suit connected with nothing more than a black metal circle centered on her navel. She added thigh-high stockings secured by garters to the suit and a pair of red leather spiked heels.

She left her hair down and her luxurious auburn curls flowed softly over her shoulders to rest on her chest. Her makeup was applied to perfection – not a flaw to be found. She over-exaggerated and enlarged her emerald green eyes, highlighted her sharp cheekbones, and painted her lips a vivid red to match her shoes.

She stood, hands on hips with a wicked smile on her face, legs slightly spread, and watched as he began to drool. As he stood there, he could do nothing but stare, unable to find the words to convey his thoughts, feelings, and excitement over the surprise she'd given him.

They'd had multiple conversations since the day they'd reunited about what they each liked, wanted, and were interested in for their sex life. They'd slowly added some of those elements, bringing mutual satisfaction, but Blaze had never given thought to Lexi taking a step like this. The knowledge that she'd give herself to him this way suddenly brought him to his knees.

As he dropped to the plush carpet, he looked up at her in awe and realized he was more in love with her than he'd ever thought possible. The love and trust she had for him and in him by offering herself this way stole the breath from his body.

"Lexi..."

With a sexual sway to her hips, she slowly walked toward him, her smile growing as mischief danced in her eyes.

"I thought I was supposed to be the one on my knees?"

"When? How?"

"Oh, that's just going to remain my little secret."

"Are you sure about all of this, Angel?" Blaze knew what a big step this was for her. Letting go, letting someone else take charge, take control, was a huge step for her. There had been a time in her life when she'd trusted nobody and had only found solace in depending on herself. She'd lost her fiance, her parents, and her sense of direction. She'd walked away from a burgeoning career where superstardom had been on the horizon. She'd hidden, closing out the world around her, and had not trusted in anyone or counted on anyone until Blaze had come along.

Being the one to make all the decisions, the only one to guide and direct her life, the only one she could depend on, had been lonely and draining. Over the time that they'd been together, she'd slowly begun to share those burdens and decisions with him. It had taken a while, even after they'd declared their love for each other, for her to realize that she didn't have to do it all by herself any longer, that he was and wanted to be her partner in every aspect.

Giving up her sense of control in the bedroom and in their sex life was yet another major leap for her, as well as for their relationship.

"Blaze," she held out a hand to him and he took it, rising so they could look at each other, eye to eye, "the only thing I'm more sure of right now is my love for you. I want to do this for you, with you, for us. I want to share in your desires and fulfill a few of my own. I've told you before that I'm yours, now I'm showing you exactly who I belong to."

His lips quickly claimed hers and his arms snaked around her voluptuous curves, molding her to him as he devoured her mouth. He had no idea how he'd gotten so lucky or what hand of fate had decided he deserved the woman he held, but he was eternally grateful. Now, with his cock straining behind the zipper of his jeans, he was determined to show Lexi just how grateful he could be.

As Blaze kissed her, Lexi felt the room begin to spin. He'd always shown her how much he wanted her, but the unabashed hunger he devoured her with made her feel wanton, vital, and cherished, all at the same time.

She'd been planning this for a while. Seeing Blaze brought to his knees had been worth the time and effort she'd put into keeping her project a secret. The look on his face when he'd opened the door had sent a thrill zinging through her body and it had taken every ounce of control she had to stay where she was and let him look around at the changes she'd made.

When they'd first gotten together she'd been curious about his sexual wants, needs, and desires. And when he'd slowly introduced her to his kinkier side, she'd gone willingly. Now, with the addition of a playroom, she knew they would be diving deeper into their explorations, and the excitement she felt was unparalleled.

Over time, she'd discovered that there was a level of pain for her that brought her untold pleasure. Blaze, knowing her heart, mind, body, and soul, knew the exact level she needed to reach ecstasy. He knew her thresholds and would only take her as far as she needed without pushing her past her limits. For him, it wasn't about inflicting pain. No, for him, it was all about giving her what she needed to reach her pleasure pinnacle. And while there were some things she didn't think she would ever be interested in, light bondage, spanking, and toys, were top of her list for sexual gratification.

He was a giving lover, always making her orgasm multiple times before he even began to physically pleasure himself and she was excited to see just what he intended with their new additions. The possibilities were endless.

His lips left hers and with a ravishing hunger she'd never before seen in his eyes, he slowly began to back her toward the cross. Her pussy began to throb in anticipation and when she felt her skin brush up against the cool metal, she began to tremble in anticipation.

He grabbed her left hand and brought it to his lips, kissing the back of it before raising it to secure it in the black cuff. He repeated the gesture with her right hand and when her wrists were secure, he gave the restraints a tug to test them. Then he smiled, satisfied that the cuffs would do their job without causing her harm. He kissed her once more, running his tongue across her lips as they parted for him, and he teased her with the slightest dip of his tongue before quickly pulling away.

Bending down, he picked up one leather-clad foot and admired the way the red contrasted against her skin. The sexy shape of her calf drew him and he licked her slowly, sensually from ankle to knee before doing the same to her other leg. Then he spread her legs so he could secure her ankles to the cross. From his position between her legs, he looked up and growled deeply as he realized he was at eye level with her pussy lips, and her arousal was slowly leaking from her body, glistening in the soft light of the room.

His tongue darted out, licking along her seam ever so slowly. Her nipples, already puckered and ready, came to hard, stiff peaks as he teased her to the point of insanity. Then he chuckled and rose to his feet, giving each nipple a quick lick before walking over to the trunk of toys.

"Well, damn, Angel, I hardly know where to begin." He pulled out a vibrator and turned it on to test it. When it lit up and began to buzz, he looked over at her with his crooked grin and wiggled his eyebrows enticingly. Then he turned his back to her and began to go through everything she'd added to the box.

At last, he walked back across the room to her, stripping out of his muscle-hugging T-shirt as he went. The sight of his naked chest always made her drool and this time was no different. There's just something, she thought, about a sexy man with a beard, muscles, and tattoos.

As he stood before her, he asked, even though she'd already answered him once, "Are you certain?"

"Yes, God, yes, and if you don't touch me soon I may lose my mind."

He leaned forward, brushing his chest against her breasts, and whispered in her ear, "Oh, I'm going to touch you, but you're going to have to be patient."

She gasped as he began licking a trail down her throat. His tongue laved against her skin until he was at the thin strip of material between her breasts. Then with a wicked gleam in his eyes, he glanced up at her as his mouth hovered over her nipple, his warm breath making her body arch forward as she waited eagerly for him to continue. Once again he growled deeply as he latched on, sucking the hard bud into his mouth and teasing the tip with his tongue.

Finally, he released her nipple and once again blew air on it. Then he pulled a silver chain from his pocket. On either end was a nipple clamp and Lexi groaned excitedly. He placed the rubber tips of the claw clamp on her nipple and tightened the sliding bead to hold it in place. "More?" He asked, and she nodded her head for him to make it tighter. She gasped as the claw pinched down even more and when he asked if she was alright, she assured him she was good.

He placed the second clamp on her other nipple and tightened it, as well. Then with her body spread, and her breasts chained together, her nipples throbbing and darkening from the pinch of the clamps, he stood back and looked her up and down. The admiration on his face sent shivers up and down her spine.

He reached for the button on his jeans, unfastened it, and then slowly lowered the zipper. Going commando was his standard so when his cock sprang forward, Lexi found herself licking her lips at the sight. Grinning, he pushed the jeans down over his thick, muscular thighs and stepped out of them before approaching her once more.

"You look like you need something, Angel." With the tips of his fingers, he softly brushed the globes of her breasts, down to her rib cage, and back up. Then with one finger he hooked the chain attached to her nipples and tugged softly. She moaned with pleasure and he tugged a little harder. Her body arched off the cross, her back bowed and she began to pant as greedy lust made her arousal begin to slowly trickle from her body and down her legs.

"More?"

"Yes, please. Yes!"

"Lower your head, Lexi, and open your mouth." She did as he asked and he placed the chain between her teeth. "Now. You can control your pain, your pleasure. Don't drop it." Teasing, he stepped away from her and her eyes darted around the room as she wondered what he had planned next. He walked to the trunk and returned only a moment later. The objects he held made her squirm – anticipation, excitement, uncertainty – they all warred within.

A silver bullet vibrator with a remote was up next in his arsenal, and with a cheeky grin on his face, he turned it on its lowest setting, then trailed it up the inside of one thigh and down the other. Over and over he did it, getting closer to her center with each pass. Just when she thought he was going to keep teasing her, he ran the buzzing toy through her pussy, coating it in her hot arousal. Then just before he touched her clit he paused, waiting until she looked up at him. With their gazes locked, he pressed the vibrator to her protruding nub. Immediately, her eyes glazed over and her body began to convulse. She tilted her head back to absorb the sensations and when she did, she found herself tugging on the chain, tugging on her nipples. The pleasure and pain sent her into an orgasmic haze.

Before she came down, he pushed the silver bullet into her, nestling it against her G-spot, and then increased the vibration speed. She wasn't sure how much more she could take as her body began to tremble uncontrollably. When she raised her head and opened her eyes once more, it was with the knowledge that this man, this incredible man, was going to give her more pleasure than he'd ever given her before.

In his hand was a small black leather flogger, the perfect size for playful fun. He snapped the soft tendrils of the flogger against his hand a few times getting the feel for the instrument. As he did, his stiff cock bounced excitedly. He came to her then and with a gentle hand, lightly and playfully flicked the flogger down against one thigh and back up the other. Then he repeated the pattern, but when he made the second path, he continued up until the flogger brushed up against her breast and then back down, teasing her nipples with a hint more pain.

Again he repeated the pattern until he set up a rhythm, gradually applying more force to his strikes. Clouded from pleasure, her eyes glazed over and she gasped, dropping the chain in her ecstasy. With a deep growl, he dropped to his knees before her and took her in his mouth. His tongue lapped up her arousal, the remnants of her first orgasm, and tantalized her clit in the same up-and-down pattern he'd used with the flogger.

When she moaned his name, he sucked her clit in his mouth and circled it with his tongue until he felt her body begin to convulse once more. Then, unable to take it any longer, he pulled the vibrator from her body and standing, plunged his cock inside her. With her body still in the throes of her second orgasm, he held still, absorbing the sensation of her walls as they convulsed around him, a massaging pulse that made him moan deeply. And while he waited for her to come down, he released her nipples from the clamps. Her breath hissed as each tortured nipple found its freedom, the shock of the return of blood flow sending a surge of euphoria tingling throughout her body.

And when she was free of the clamps, he placed tender kisses on the abused skin to ease her soreness, gently licking each nipple and worshipping her body. Then he held her head in his hands until her glazed eyes locked on his once more.

"With me this time, Angel. Come with me. This time, we go together."

He kissed her then, tongue diving inside her mouth and warring with hers as he began to move. With long, slow strokes he fucked her, basking in her tightness. Then as her body began to loosen once more, as she relaxed and opened herself for him, he began to move faster, pounding harder. Building his speed, his stiff cock throbbed as he filled her time and again. Then, reaching his limits, he moved his hands down her body to her hips. Holding her in place, he lost what little control he'd been able to hold onto from the moment he'd opened the bedroom door.

His hips pistoned his cock inside her and the faster he pounded, the faster he climbed the incline into oblivion. She kept pace with him, her body climbing in tandem with his, until with a primal roar, he reached the final peak and fell into a sea of bliss, pulling her with him. They both gasped for air as they went over then under and their bodies stilled as he filled her, pumping her full of his cum as her body milked his cock for each and every drop of his essence.

Chapter Five

Lexi was only vaguely aware of Blaze pulling out of her and beginning to remove her restraints. She remembered her knees going weak and him scooping her into his arms. She remembered the feel of her head resting on his shoulder as he carried her down the hall to their room and wrapped a blanket around her. After that, she remembered nothing until she woke in their bed enveloped in his arms with him softly snoring in her ear, his breath tickling her neck with each exhale.

Smiling as she thought about their time in what she now thought of as their adult Toys-R-Us, she snuggled closer to him, tugging his arm more tightly around her waist and pushing her butt against the morning erection that strained between them. Her body was tender, but the soreness was pleasing, a gentle reminder that letting go and giving Blaze control was a very, very good thing.

His breathing changed with her movements and he shifted his body to press his stiff cock against her.

"Mmmm. Good morning, Angel."

"It is definitely a good morning." She smiled and scraped her teeth across her bottom lip as she considered. "Shall we make it a better morning?"

He chuckled at her suggestion. "You don't think maybe you're a little too sore for that?"

"Possibly, but we'll never know until we try." She reached between them and wrapped her hand around his cock, giving him a little squeeze. He groaned at the feel of her hand pleasuring him. Then checking to see how wet she was, how ready for him she was, he gave in to temptation, to her seduction, and took her from behind. Time had no meaning as he loved her gently, as their bodies gave each other the sweetest of pleasures once more.

After their morning love-making, they showered and headed downstairs to prepare breakfast. Now, they sat with pancakes and bacon piled on their plates and steaming mugs of coffee giving them a boost as they got caught up on the events of the day before. For Blaze, it was one of his favorite times of day – morning, in his opinion, offered so many possibilities and he cherished each new beginning he was given with the woman he loved.

"How were things down at the site yesterday? Are we on track?"

"Everything looks good. They poured the concrete for the last building and everything is really starting to come together." Excitement filled her voice as she continued. "I did what I hope was the last of the interviews for camp director and hired two more instructors. I can't believe how far we've come and how quickly everything has progressed. It's almost scary how easily it has all fallen into place."

"I'm so damn glad, Angel. So, do you think you've got a good candidate for the director position?"

"Yes, actually, I do. And while he doesn't have much experience with music other than listening to it, he more than meets all my other requirements. He's an Eagle Scout, camp and wilderness trained, has successfully run a scouting program for several years in Georgia, and by all appearances, is good with teenagers. He has all his certificates, first aid, CPR, etcetera, and comes highly recommended by his work and personal references."

"Will his lack of musical abilities be a problem?'

"I really don't think so. I need someone to run the camp, set schedules, and make sure that things flow smoothly. The classes and lessons will be left in the hands of the instructors. If he accepts the position, I think it will be an excellent fit."

A soft whine had both of them looking down to where Lucky lay, head on paws, glancing back and forth between Blaze and Lexi, waiting patiently for any morsel of food to be dropped or tossed his way.

"Awe! Are ya hungry, big guy?" Lexi held out a piece of bacon and the dog gently took it from her before devouring it in one gulp and looking back up at her with adoring eyes pleading for more.

"Spoiled. He's completely spoiled." Blaze shook his head at the innocent look on Lucky's face.

Lexi smiled and began to rub the dog's head, a sign of solidarity, and Lucky responded by laying his head in her lap for more attention.

"Who would have thought my biggest competition for your affections would be a dog?" Blaze grinned cheekily at her as he popped the last bite of breakfast in his mouth.

"Oh, speaking of competition, I sort of got hit on by the new site foreman yesterday."

Blaze stilled and raised an eyebrow in question. "Excuse me?"

The bell tone of Lexi's laugh echoed throughout the kitchen. "Yeah, he seemed disappointed that not only did I have a significant other, but that I'm engaged. I think he was hoping he had a chance. And I mean, he's a nice enough looking guy..." She trailed off as the growl that rippled from deep within Blaze's chest made Lexi's eyes alight with mischief. "Now, I wonder why having you go all caveman over some guy hitting on me just sent shivers down my spine?"

"You're playing with fire, Angel."

"I've told you before, I can handle the heat as long as it's your flames licking at me."

"Well, look who's feeling sassy this morning. Now that you've set up a playroom for us, we may have to see just how much of that heat you really can handle."

Red tinged Lexi's cheeks and her breath caught. "I'm looking forward to it."

"Now, back to this foreman. Do I need to have a word with him?"

"Oh, Blaze! No!" She laughed, "It wasn't like that. It was very innocent and he came off as just curious. As soon as I told him that I was unavailable, he changed the subject and then went back to work."

"Okay. But you let me know if you think I need to make an appearance down there."

"Good grief. You know getting hit on is nothing new for me. It's flattering, but not a big deal. Besides, you're the only man I want. So don't think you need to go down there flashing your muscles with guns locked and loaded. It isn't necessary."

Blaze took a deep breath and nodded his head in agreement. "Alright. But if something changes, I'm the first to know, okay?"

Lexi grinned and then saluted, "Yes, Sir!"

"Sassy. Definitely sassy. I love it!" Rising, he gathered his dirty dishes and took them to the sink. "I need to head out." Walking back to where she sat, he leaned down and kissed her goodbye, lingering for just a moment. Then, giving Lucky a quick pat on the head he commanded, "Take care of my angel until I get back."

A 'woof' of agreement from Lucky, a quick wink at Lexi, and he was out the door.

When Blaze walked in the door of the police station he was greeted by Ms. Eliza who waited beside his desk with a cup of coffee and a pecan pie – wrapped with a pretty red bow atop. Everybody, it seemed, knew of his unabashed love for pecan pie.

"Good morning, Ms. Eliza. Now, what's all this?" Blaze grinned at the elderly woman even as his mouth began to water in anticipation of having a slice with his lunch.

"Just a little thank you for all your help yesterday. In all my years of driving this is the first time that I've ever been involved in an accident. And even though I've dealt with things on this side hundreds of times, I sort of lost my head when it happened to me. I swear on my granny's grave I could not think of what steps I needed to take. I appreciate you stepping in and taking over. You sure made my life a bit easier."

"Awe, now. I was just doing my job."

"And rightly so. But in my opinion, you went above and beyond. Above and beyond gets pie."

With that, she placed the pie on his desk and walked away leaving Blaze grinning after her.

"Well, damn, son. She doesn't do that for just any-one. She must like you." Sheriff Kaminski chuckled as the leaned an arm on the privacy divider surrounding Blaze's desk. "It's the tattoos, isn't it? You can tell me. Women just love a man with tattoos." A snort sounded from across the room at this statement and Blaze looked over in time to see Deputy Shaver roll his eyes before returning his attention to whatever he was working on at his desk.

"You going to keep giving me a hard time or tell me what's in that folder?" Blaze grinned cheekily up at his superior.

"Just taking all the fun out of it for me, aren't ya? Well, be that way." Handing Blaze the file, the Sheriff continued, "We've gotten a couple of reports of some drug dealers trying to peddle their wares around the school, the park, and a couple of other local teen hangout spots. I don't think they're going to be difficult to catch, but I'm afraid they're part of something bigger. I wanted to run some thoughts by you, and get your ideas on some surveillance."

"Damn. What are they dealing?"

"So far, mostly weed and prescription drugs, but late last night we got a call from a mom who had cleaned out her kid's gym bag and found what she thinks is cocaine. I've sent it off to the lab to be analyzed. All the kid could say was that he'd been skateboarding over at the park after school yesterday and a guy, mid to late twenties or so, tall, lanky, dark hair, scruffy beard but otherwise clean, approached him to give him a sample. Kid swears up and down that he was going to give it to his parents to turn it in, but put it in his bag and forgot about it until his mother found it and threatened the wrath of God."

"Sure he was."

"Yeah. I wasn't born yesterday. Anyway, if you've got some time, let's brainstorm and see what we can come up with. I want to get this nipped before it gets worse."

"Absolutely."

Lexi hit send on the email she'd just finished and leaned back in her chair and grinned. Then, with a small squeal of celebration, she pushed against her desk and sent her office chair spinning while she pumped her fists in the air. Her newly hired camp director had enthusiastically accepted her offer and quickly signed his paperwork. With that addition, she had a full camp staff in place and could concentrate her efforts on her music for the remainder of the day.

Her mind had raced all morning with bits and pieces, little snippets of lines that she wanted to put together to see what she could forge into a song. Her time with Blaze the night before had been just the release she'd needed, and though he'd clouded her mind once more that morning, she'd entered the day with a clear head and racing thoughts. It will be interesting, she thought, to see just what might come from their night together.

She looked down to where Lucky had popped up from his nap when she'd squealed and grinned at him. "How about we go out so you can get a little run in before I bury myself in the studio?" With a happy woof and quick spin of his own, he followed her out the door and down the stairs. As she walked out on the back deck and leaned on the railing to watch as the dog stretched his legs, she couldn't help but take advantage of the beautiful day. Warm sunshine smiled down on her and though the air was still cool, the breeze that ruffled the leaves was gentle and calm.

She patted the railing, setting a familiar rhythm and when she began to belt out one of her songs, happiness spread throughout her body and pulsed from her soul. Her rich alto echoed throughout the stillness and brought the wandering dog back to the railing to stare up at her in adoration. She worked her way through the song then as the last note faded, she took just a moment to appreciate the way the sound floated away along the airwaves. She would never, she thought, absolutely never take the gift of her music for granted again. It was too precious to think of so lightly.

Funny, she thought as she looked out across her yard, how when you were truly in love everything took on new depths. Songs had more meaning, food tasted better, the brush of a hand could envelop you in loving warmth, and a simple word spoken at just the right moment could send you soaring. Blaze had done that to her repeatedly. There were times when he was moving in her, eyes locked with hers, lost in the magic they made together and he would whisper a plea of "now" and she would come undone. And there were times when those words were more than a plea, they were a command spoken with an urgency that would send her flying into submission.

She laughed at herself for getting lost in her thoughts. "Well, that'll get the creative juices flowing!"

She leaned over and reached out a hand to pet the dog then suddenly found herself pausing as a shiver prickled the hair on her neck and sent tingles of wariness down her spine. She jerked upright and quickly scanned the yard looking for anything amiss. Her heart began to beat faster as she searched the grounds and wondered what had caused her to feel concerned. While it wouldn't be too uncommon to have the occasional black bear wander through, she didn't plan on being outside to confront one when it did. But she found nothing out of place and seeing no danger, slowly began to let her guard down once more.

"C'mon, Lucky. Let's go inside. We have work to do anyway."

She stepped inside the house, then with a final curious look around the yard, closed and locked the door.

Blaze reached for the cup of lukewarm coffee sitting in his console and grimaced as he took a drink. He'd been sitting in his truck for the better part of an hour keeping surveillance on the town park. Kids had come and gone during that time span, doing the typical teen activities. Skateboarding seemed to be one of their favored pastimes and seeing the kids doing flips and tricks on their boards made him think of his own teen years.

He hadn't been nearly as good as these kids appeared to be, but he hadn't been half bad. Still, the thought of getting on one of the boards now made him cringe. The teenager inside him wanted to say he could still do it, but the thirty-year-old man currently feeling the aches and pains of sitting on his ass in one spot for too long laughed uproariously.

Oh well, he thought, he had much more physically pleasing activities now. A mental picture of Lexi secured to the cross the night before flashed through his mind and when it did, he felt his heart flip in his chest. He simply couldn't begin to fathom how he'd gotten so lucky. Yeah, he'd been through his hell before he'd found his little piece of heaven, but even with all he'd been through, all he'd participated in as part of his duty to his country, he wouldn't change anything.

Well, he grimaced, knowing that was not entirely true. If he could have changed the outcome of the insurgency that had ultimately caused the loss of his dearest friend, he would have done that. Still, he tried to keep in mind that the tiny life he'd saved in the process deserved a chance to live and become, whereas his friend had known the dangers of his enlistment. After months and months of therapy, he'd finally come to terms with the decisions that he'd made that day. And while it still hurt to know that he'd not been there to protect his friend, to keep his friend safe, he knew that ultimately he'd made the right choice. The guilt was still there, but he knew that if he was ever faced with that kind of situation again, he'd make the same decision.

He scanned the park once more and noted that the sun had begun to set. Soon all the remaining kids would be heading home for the evening and that was exactly where he was ready to go himself. Knowing that Lexi waited at home for him made the long days away from her a bit easier to bear. And while part of him wanted to be by her side every minute of every day, he knew they both needed some space, some time apart from each other. Having that separation just helped him to appreciate his time together with her even more.

Out of the corner of his eye, he saw a car turn the corner opposite of the park and slowly drive by before turning at the next corner and continuing onto Main Street and out of sight. Interesting. He was fairly certain that car had made a drive-by not long after he'd parked and begun his surveillance. He made note of the make and model and then decided that it was time to head back to the station, type up his notes, and see if there was anything urgent waiting at his desk. He revved his truck to life and drove the short distance to the Sheriff's office to finish out his day.

As he sat down at his computer and logged in he saw the voicemail light on his phone flashing, a warning beacon that for some unknown reason instantly filled him with dread. With trepidation, he picked up the receiver, pushed the lighted button, and entered his personal code to retrieve whatever messages awaited him. When he found not one, but two hang-up calls, he tried not to let his mind begin to assume the worst. Instead, he logged the calls, noting the date and time, and then turned to his computer, typed up his report, and emailed it to Sheriff Kaminski. Then he logged off and with a final glance at his call log, grabbed the remainder of the pecan pie and headed home.

Chapter Six

F our days later Blaze and the Sheriff sat in his truck down the road from the high school and watched a lone figure leaning against a tree on the corner adjacent to the school. Huddled in a bulky coat and puffing on a cigarette, he waited, eyes darting left and right as he did so, for the kids to come streaming from the school at the end of the day. They'd seen him there three days in a row and though they hadn't observed him approaching any of the children yet, they knew it was only a matter of time.

Each day they'd taken turns following him and each day he'd slowly meandered to the park after the kids had cleared out. They could have gone to him at any time and run him off, but knowing that he was at least a part of the drug ring they looked to take down, they patiently waited for him to dig his own hole. Day by day he'd gotten antsier as he'd paced and leaned, paced and leaned, and then done the same at the park.

"It'll be today."

"I agree." Sheriff Kaminski looked over at Blaze with pride. He'd seen something in Blaze from the first time he'd laid eyes on him. Somehow he'd just known that Blaze was needed within the department and he was grateful that he'd put the idea of joining the force into his head. They'd hit it off right away and now he not only considered him an exemplary employee and great friend but also a bit of a surrogate son. "He can't wait too long between deals. He'll have the next level in the chain breathing down his neck if he does. He's gotta bring that money in with some kind of regularity or he'll get cut loose. Or just cut. Maybe both."

"Yeah, and he hasn't gotten a sale here and from what I've observed at the park he hasn't gotten one there, either. It's time."

Three-thirty hit and within seconds the doors opened and teenagers hurriedly filed out, some walking to their cars, some heading toward busses, and some on foot as they began to walk toward the center of town to hang out at the park or over at Ma's for an afternoon snack. Teen boys laughed and joked while doing the normal push and shove of comradery. Teen girls giggled behind their hands at the shenanigans of the boys they were crushing on, and a few couples strolled behind all of them, hand-in-hand, lazily taking their time and stealing a chaste kiss or two.

But these weren't the kids that the dealer was looking for and he bided his time as the various groups passed him by. At last, his target audience began to appear – the loners, the kids that didn't quite fit in, the kids that had hit puberty and weren't handling it well, lost in their misery. The kids looking for an escape, looking for a way to forget their problems, a way to make sense of what they were feeling and thinking - those were the kids that he looked to hook.

A boy of about fifteen walked by the tree where the dealer waited and had barely passed when he straightened from his pose and called to the kid. The boy paused and looked back then started to walk again, but the dealer was persistent, and the boy eventually stopped to talk.

Blaze and the Sheriff waited with their hands on the door handles of the truck. Timing would be key. As soon as they saw the dealer reach in an inside pocket and pull a packet out they quietly exited the truck and gently pushed the doors to. Walking stealthily, they began to work their way toward the deal.

The kid caught their movement and his eyes widened as he realized what was about to happen. The dealer, back turned to where Blaze and the Sheriff approached,

looked over his shoulder quickly and seeing them, panicked and began to run. Blaze didn't hesitate. Instincts
and training kicked in and he took off after the dealer,
running as fast as could. When he heard the Sheriff yell
encouragement at his efforts, he laughed gleefully.

"Run, Forrest! Run!"

The dealer was fast, but he was no competition for
Blaze. One hundred yards of minimal effort and Blaze
caught up to him. Leaping, he tackled him to the ground
and rolled with him once, twice, before burying his face
in the grass and yanking his arms behind his back to cuff
him.

Blaze jerked him up and recited Miranda rights as he
began perp walking him back to where the Sheriff stood
talking to the kid. "You have the right to remain silent.
Now whether you have the brains to do so or not remains to be seen. Anything you say can and will be used
against you in a court of law. You have the right to speak
to an attorney, and to have an attorney present when
we question you about your activities. If you can't afford
one – and by looking at the knockoff shit you're wearing
I'm going to assume you can't - one will be provided for
you. Those guys are called public defenders. If you're
lucky you'll get one who will do a good job for you. If
not, you may get the opportunity to be someone's bitch
in the slammer. Have fun with that. Do you understand
your rights?"

"Fuck you!"

"Thanks, but I'll pass." Blaze smirked as he continued, "I have a beautiful lady waiting for me at home that I much prefer to fuck."

"Deputy..." Sheriff Kaminski shook his head and grinned at him even as he censured him. "Be nice to our new friend, now. We're going to be spending quite a bit of time getting to know each other and we want him to be in a forthcoming mood."

"You got it, Sheriff."

An hour later they sat in the conference room at the police station talking with the kid and his parents.

"Thank you both for intervening. It looks like we are going to be having some long talks when we get home." The mom looked back and forth between Blaze and the Sheriff. "And you," she turned to look pleadingly at her child, "need to thank them, as well."

"Mom, I promise I wasn't going to take anything!"

"Quiet." The dad gave his son a stern look and the kid quickly closed his mouth and swallowed the objections that he'd been spewing from the moment they'd brought him into the station.

"Y'all can head on out. We've got his statement. If we need anything further, we'll be in touch."

Blaze watched as the Sheriff walked them to the door and shook hands with the parents. Once they were gone he turned back and grinned mischievously.

"You ready for some fun?"

"Always."

"Well then, go get that asshole out of the cell and let's get started." Blaze reached into his pocket and pulled out his keys as he walked toward the back of the station.

"So, I guess you're good cop?"

"Son. I've always been a good cop. You'll get there one of these days."

"Funny."

"I try. But to answer your question, yes, I'll take the nice road, you take the snarky. You excel with the snark."

Blaze chuckled at their banter, "I try."

"Let's start from the beginning, shall we?" Sheriff Kaminski looked across the table to where the drug dealer sat. Cuffed to the arm of the rickety chair he occupied, he leered across the table at his interrogators. When no response came, the Sheriff shook his head. "Talkative, aren't ya?"

"I can get him to talk." Blaze rubbed his hands together in a menacing and somewhat threatening manner. "Five minutes and he'll be singing an octave higher and spilling his secrets."

"Now, Blaze. I've told you before. Don't antagonize the prisoners."

"Just stating facts, Sir."

"Be that as it may, let's see if we can have a simple conversation and avoid drastic measures."

"As you wish." The Sheriff cocked an eyebrow at Blaze in amusement as he recognized Blaze's attempt at humor with his movie reference.

"As I said in the beginning, Mr. Johnson, we have you on several charges: possession of illegal drugs and paraphernalia, including Cocaine, LSD, Fentanyl, and Heroin, possession with intent to sell said drugs, and then there's the fact that you were doing all this within very close proximity of a school zone. Does that sound about right to you?"

The dealer shrugged his shoulders and continued staring off to the side.

"Look, kid. We've heard it all before. You have no idea where the drugs came from. You found them. You just wanted to make a little extra cash. It's bullshit and we all know it's bullshit. We know you're not top-tier, so how about giving us a name?"

The dealer's knee started bouncing up and down but still, he didn't speak.

When the dealer continued to remain silent, Blaze walked around the table and sat on the edge facing him. Looking down at him with a sneer, Blaze pointed to a long, slicing scar on his arm. "I know I'm paraphrasing here, but you should know, '*I have a very particular set of skills, skills I have acquired over a very long career, skills that make me a nightmare for people like you.*' You see this? I got this taking down a drug lord in Columbia. You see this," he pointed to another scar on the inside of his palm, "I got this when his brother tried to take me out. Guess what? I won. I always win. One way or another, you're going down. The question is, are you taking this walk by yourself or are you taking a friend with you?"

"Blaze..."

"I'm just pointing out that I'm not going to stop until whoever he's working for is sitting exactly where he is. Or, in the morgue. I'm good with either of those options."

"Deputy!"

"Fine." Blaze walked back around to the other side of the table and sat next to the Sheriff.

"Now, let's start again, shall we?"

By the time they exited the interview, they didn't have much more to go on than they'd had when they began the interrogation. Blaze escorted the prisoner back to a holding cell, and when he returned to the office, walked over to the Sheriff's desk for a recap.

"He hasn't cried lawyer yet, but he will."

"Yeah, and if he doesn't, we're not going to have much time before the public defender's office steps in. He's little league, Blaze. The question is how many levels are we going to have to climb before we hit the major leagues and take down the big boss?"

"My guess would be that there's only one other level – locally anyway, and once we're past that, we're going to have to turn everything over to the Feds."

"Fuck. I know. It sure would be nice to be able to call them up and tell them we have a present for them all tied up in a pretty red bow."

"We'll keep after him, Sheriff. I think if we give him a night in the cell before we try again, we might get some-where. You can tell he wants to talk. He's just fucking scared."

"I can't blame him. I guess we'll have to wait and see if he caves or if he's tougher than he looks." Stephen hit a button on his computer and the screen went dark. "Let's shut it down for the night and come back to it with fresh eyes in the morning."

"Sounds good."

"Nice job today, Deputy."

Blaze watched as the Sheriff walked out the front door, then wandered over to his desk and started to shut his computer down. When he noticed his message light was blinking once again, he reluctantly retrieved the messages. He found two more hang-up calls and his intuition began to spark. Somehow, he knew there was going to be more to the calls than something as simple as a wrong number.

And knowing that, he began to run through possibility after possibility. By the time he left, he had a lengthy list and he found he didn't care for any of the scenarios that popped into his mind – not a single one.

With a clothes basket of freshly washed laundry in her arms, Lexi walked out the back door and glanced up at the sunny sky. Not a cloud in sight, she thought and began to ready her clothesline so she could hang the laundry to dry. The retractable line ran from the deck to one of the tall maple trees on the edge of the property, and she loved to use it as often as possible. Grabbing the metal ring attached to the end of the line, she walked down the stairs and out into the yard pulling as she went. When she reached the tree, she secured the ring in the large utility hook deeply embedded in the hard-wood of the tree and began to fill the line, one garment at a time.

As she worked, the dog roamed and sniffed, and she sang, belting out classic country songs while she let memories of her years growing up in Kentucky take her back in time. She'd been fortunate to have the parents she had and to grow up in such a small town. They'd lived close enough to the Land Between the Lakes recreational area that they'd often gone camping and fishing. Her love of the outdoors and nature had been instilled in her when she was very young. Her love of country music had also been instilled in her very young. And while she loved all different types of music, it was always country that pulled at her heart.

Music had been a staple in her house. Her mother would turn the radio on every morning and it would stay on until they went to bed. Singing had come naturally and when she'd discovered just how good her voice was, it was as if all the stars had aligned for her and opened a path to her future.

Thinking back to those years, she couldn't help but think of her parents, of Jackson and the future that they'd planned together. When she lost all of them, she'd hidden behind her pain. She closed herself off from her music, and for the most part, had closed herself off from the world. Now she wondered if her mother would have been disappointed in her for turning away from her music. She liked to think she would have understood and would have been happy and proud of her for finally being able to open herself back up to the world around her.

I wonder, she thought as she placed the last piece of clothing on the line, just what my parents would think of Blaze? She smiled as she imagined their reactions.

The snapping of a twig echoed loudly in the stillness of the morning, and Lucky barked at the sound. Lexi's head popped up in surprise and quickly turned in the direction of the intrusive noise. Her heart raced as she listened closely and looked around for movement. When the sound didn't repeat and Lucky made no further reaction, she began to calm down. With a shake of her head at her jumpiness, she picked up her empty clothes basket and returned to the sanctuary of the house.

Chapter Seven

L exi spent the remainder of the morning writing a new song. Knowing her ability to lose track of everything when she was absorbed in her music, she set an alarm to alert her when it was closing in on time for the next to-do item for the day. When the warning tone sounded, she jumped and then laughed at herself, startled by the noise that had pulled her out of her artistic zone. She'd been so involved in the words she was writing, in the music she was creating, that she completely lost track of how much time had passed.

Now, she took a deep breath and braced herself for the Zoom meeting she had scheduled. This meeting would be the first time that all of her employees would be introduced to each other and she hoped their personalities meshed as well as she had originally thought they would. It was imperative they were all on the same page as far as the kids, the program, and how to handle any potential issues as they arose.

Over the past couple of weeks, she'd worked with the instructors one-on-one to help formulate lessons that were educational and instructional, but fun. She didn't want the campers to feel as if they were still in school – this was still the kids' summer vacation, after all. The whole point of the camp was not only to give private instruction to the kids, but to teach them to find music in and around them, no matter where they might be, and, above all, to have fun while doing it.

So far, the idea of the camp had been met with a positive reception. She'd given interview after interview, television, newspapers, websites – she'd made the rounds to promote her new venture. People seemed to like the idea and hoped that it would help to bring revenue to the area. She'd advertised locally at first and, within the last month, had begun to branch out regionally. It was her hope that one day she would be able to take the camp to national status and make it an elite and sought-after location to send budding musicians.

The future, she thought, was wide open.

Glancing at the clock and seeing that it was time to begin, she closed her eyes and crossed her fingers. Then, opening one eye in trepidation and saying a quick prayer, she clicked on the link. Then squaring her shoulders and turning on her innate charm, she entered the meeting and welcomed her team to the first of many brainstorming sessions.

Two hours later she clicked off the meeting and jumped from her chair with excitement. She pumped her fists in the air and squealed as she shook her ass in a happy dance of celebration.

"Lucky!" The dog, who had jumped up and started barking in celebration right along with her, stopped and looked up at her with his tongue lolling out of the side of his mouth as he yipped in excitement. "I did it! We did it! It's going to be absolutely amazing and everything that I hoped it would be! Aggh! I'm so damn excited!"

"Woof!"

"Alright, come on buddy. You've been cooped up here too long. You've got to be about to bust a gut. Let's head outside for a minute and take a little break!" She started toward the door and was beaten there by the dog who raced ahead of her happily.

By the time she reached the back door, he was there patiently waiting for her to open his gateway to doggy heaven and she laughed as she saw his butt wiggling and tail wagging in anticipation. "I'm here! I'm here! Out with you!"

She opened the door and started to step onto the back deck but stopped in her tracks and gasped in shock when she saw the mess smeared across the hardwood of the deck. Even the dog had stopped, hackles rising as he growled low and deep and gave warning barks. "Lucky! Sit! Stay!" Though she could tell it took real effort for him to obey, he did actually listen and stayed inside the entryway to the house. She looked around quickly to make sure that the danger had passed and wasn't lurking around the edges of the property. Then seeing that everything was clear, she looked back down at the crime scene that waited on her doorstep.

"Well, that's gross. Eww!"

Blood pooled around the mutilated body of what she was finally able to determine were the remains of a rabbit. Bits of fur glued into the dried blood on the decking fluttered in the light breeze that blew across the property. Bones, sinew, and organs were scattered in a kill pattern that circled out from the point where the rabbit had met its untimely end. And lifeless eyes stared out at her from the detached head almost as if it had been placed to stare into the house at whoever opened the door.

"Alright, buddy. It's okay, Lucky. Bless it. That poor rabbit didn't have a fighting chance against whatever animal ripped it to pieces. I'm sorry, bud, but you have to stay inside until I get this cleaned up. Eww. Just...eww!"

She quickly went to the shed to grab a bucket and shovel and then walked around to the back deck. She gathered as much of the detritus as she could and carted it to the back line of the property. Digging a hole as deep as she could, she dumped the contents of the bucket and quickly covered it all, tamping down the disturbed dirt before returning to the house to clean her tools and scrub the deck.

By the time she was done, daylight had started to fade into twilight. She let the dog loose and stepped back in the house long enough to grab a bottle of beer before she walked back out on the deck and plopped down in one of her Adirondack chairs to prop her feet up. Well, that sucked, she thought, and took a deep drink from the bottle and closed her eyes as she let the magic of the alcohol begin to relax her tense shoulders.

She'd just taken her last swallow from the bottle when she heard Blaze's truck pull into the drive. She couldn't help the smile that crossed her face. It was inevitable. Just the thought of him always boosted her mood and knowing that he was about to walk through the kitchen and come to find her as she chilled out from the pressures of the day made not only her face smile but her heart as well.

"There's my beautiful Angel." He kissed the top of her head as he set a fresh bottle of beer on the table next to her. Then sitting in the chair beside her, he took a swig of his out of his own bottle and reached for her hand. "Long day?"

"Yeah. For the most part, it was good, but definitely long."

"For the most part?" He looked over at her questioningly.

"Let's just say I had some unpleasantness to deal with this afternoon." Her body shook as a shiver went down her spine as she thought of the disgusting mess she'd found.

Blaze squeezed her hand in concern. "What happened?"

By the time she'd made it through the story her throat was dry and she took another long drink from the bottle he'd brought her. "Awe, Lexi. I'm sorry you had to deal with that by yourself."

"It's alright. But I'll tell you this, it sure turned me off fixing dinner tonight."

"Well, then, how about we do something different?" He reached for her other hand then and pulled her up and over into his lap, cuddling her close and nuzzling his face against her neck.

Lexi grinned as she felt his cock start to harden in his jeans. "Blaze, that's not something different," she giggled.

"That, Angel, is involuntary. Sometimes, just a random thought about you causes it. An innocent touch as I walk past you, your scent lingering on your pillow – mmm...truthfully, it doesn't take much to turn me on when it comes to you. But, no, I was thinking that maybe we'd go out to eat. We could go to Ma's or if you want to, we could head down to Marlinton. I hear there's a new steakhouse that's opened up down there."

"Hmmm, an hour drive with the sexiest man I've ever met, one who just happens to be the love of my life? And with a hot, juicy steak at the end of our journey? I think I can handle that." She leaned down and kissed him, relishing the soft fullness of his lips. Then she pulled back just far enough to whisper against him, "Mmm...more..." and then she licked his lips sensually. He parted for her then and allowed her to take what she needed, as much as she needed, for as long as she needed.

When she turned and straddled his lap his hands automatically came to her hips and she found herself grinding against him lustfully.

"Ahh, Angel. My Angel. If you do much more of that we won't be taking that drive."

"Uh uh, this is just a teaser, an appetizer. You've promised me a steak and this girl doesn't turn down perfectly prepared meat." She grinned as she continued to grind against him. His cock grew harder and harder. "See, perfectly prepared..."

"Oh fuck." He sucked in a breath and she knew she'd gotten to him.

"Do you think you can wait? I promise to make it worth it."

"You drive a hard bargain, Lexi."

"Yeah, well, when we get home I'm going to drive you crazy. You don't mind giving me the controls, do you?"

"Hell, no. I'm all yours anytime you want. Use me, play with me, drive me insane. Just remember to hold me afterward. You know I love it when you cuddle me."

"Deal. Give me five minutes to get ready." She grinned and kissed him again before hopping up and calling the dog to her side. "Time to go in, Lucky!"

Blaze watched her disappear into the house. The smile that she naturally brought to his face quickly faded as he went back over the discovery she'd made that afternoon. She fully believed that it was an animal that had destroyed the rabbit, but he wasn't so sure. Absently he rubbed at his neck where the tingles of intuition had started prickling against his skin. Something, he thought, just wasn't right about the way she'd described the kill. Something about it seemed more like a massacre rather than a meal. But he hadn't been home to see it before she'd cleaned it up and although he understood why she went ahead and did it, he kind of wished she'd left it for him to see and take care of. Some gut instinct was telling him that trouble was coming. He had no idea what, from where, or why, but it was coming, nonetheless.

A good cop could see trouble approaching from a mile away and that's exactly what Sheriff Stephen Kaminski saw when he walked into the office the next day and looked over to where Blaze sat staring at his computer, hand on chin, and deep in thought. Curious, but concerned, he approached the desk.

"Might as well fill me in."

"Well, good morning, to you, too." Blaze glanced up and smirked with his greeting.

"You said that so nicely then had to ruin it with your face." He laughed good-naturedly. "Come on, what's changed since yesterday? Last I saw you were practically skipping out of here after that takedown and interrogation. You and Lexi having trouble?"

"Between me and Lexi? No. Nah, things are good there. In fact, things are great there."

"Awe, hell! Wipe that goofy grin off your puss. I do NOT want details!"

"Ha! You wish! No, man. Nothing between me and Lexi, but I'm afraid there's something going on. I didn't say anything, but the other day I found a couple of hangups on my voicemail. I logged it but didn't think anything more of it. Before I left last night I found two more. Then when I came in this morning there was this." Blaze pressed a key on his keyboard and a recorded voice came through his speakers – deep, brief, and slightly garbled.

'I know what you did and I'm going to make you pay for it.'

"Fuck."

"Yeah, 'fuck' pretty much covers it. And there's more. Lexi had an incident yesterday that I'm not certain adds up." He relayed the story of the mutilated rabbit and as he described the scene, Stephen's mind began to race.

"So, with that message you know I have to ask, do you have any idea what they're talking about?"

"I wish I could tell you no, but the longer I've sat here this morning, the more I think I might. There could be someone trying to mess with me from the work I've done around here. For a small town, we've tackled quite a bit over the past couple of years. Hell, it could even be related to that drug deal we fucked up yesterday when we put that dealer out of commission. But, my instincts tell me that it's more personal." He inhaled deeply before he continued, "On that personal level, there's quite a bit that this person could be talking about from my time in the special forces. But there's really only one thing that haunts me from that period in my life. There's really only one thing that someone would try to use against me. If that's what it is and not just some bullshit from taking this job, then there may be some serious trouble ahead."

"And?"

"It's classified. Records sealed."

"Shit."

"Yeah. I just reached out to my commander. It may take a while for it to go up the chain, but I've requested permission to share all that I can about the incident with you. Hell, I haven't even been able to tell Lexi but the bare minimum. She doesn't know the where, the when, or the why. That might be all I'll be able to tell you, too. I'll just have to wait and see."

"And you think the dead rabbit might have something to do with it?"

"Coincidence or completely unrelated? It's possible it's connected, but I just don't know. And I don't like taking those kinds of chances with Lexi."

"Blaze, I made you my deputy for a reason. You know what the hell you're doing; you have great instincts, knowledge, and skill. I'd put my life in your hands a hundred times over. You tell me how you want to handle it and I'll stand behind your decision."

"Thanks. I need to think on it a bit and hopefully hear back from my commander. I'll let you know. For now, let's get back to taking down this drug ring."

"Sounds good."

Chapter Eight

L exi scribbled one line and then another and then sang through what she'd written with the melody that floated through her head. Slowly she built upon what she'd already written, going back and changing a word here and there, refining and fine-tuning until she was pleased with the song she'd composed. Then she went back through what she'd done and decided it was time to fill out the melody with rich notes, octaves, and chords. Over and over she went through it, adding and taking away here and there until she had it exactly the way she wanted it.

Then, for the hell of it, she played through and sang it all one more time before going to the next step and recording it.

You crashed into my life
And tore through the dark
I gave you my heart and soul
Without you, I'd never be whole

In the dark, you gave me your light
In my chaos, you brought your calm
On my knees, I crawled
And you taught me to stand
Take my hand
Palm to palm
Take my hand
I'll be your balm
Take my hand
I know you'll understand

Bleeding and broken I waited
Never searching for more
You gave me hope
Hope I never before could afford

In the dark, you gave me your light
In my chaos, you brought your calm
On my knees, I crawled
And you taught me to stand
Take my hand
Palm to palm

Take my hand
I'll be your balm
Take my hand
I know you'll understand

You pieced my heart together
And now I want forever
I lay my heart at your feet
Without you I'm incomplete

In the dark, you gave me your light
In my chaos, you brought your calm
On my knees, I crawled
And you taught me to stand
Take my hand
Palm to palm
Take my hand
I'll be your balm
Take my hand
I know you'll understand
You'll always understand

Lexi let the last note drift away and as it faded, she breathed in deeply through her nose, held it, and then slowly released it. She rose and turned toward her equipment. Then she let out a soft squeal as she realized she was no longer alone.

"OMG! Blaze! What are you doing? Why are you home so early? You scared the daylights out of me!" He didn't speak as he continued to stand there, staring at her, not making a move, not making a sound. Worried, she started toward him. "Blaze?" Then he sniffled and blinked rapidly, shedding any trace of the tears that had welled in his eyes before they could fall.

"You wrote that about us. That song, it's... I can't find my words, Lexi. It's beautiful. You're beautiful. I want you to sing that at the wedding. Will you do that for me? Sing for me that day?"

She wrapped her arms around his waist and laid her head on his shoulder as he enveloped her in the warmth of his strong arms. "Of course, I will. I'll sing to you anytime you want, but especially on our wedding day."

They stood there holding onto each other, simply being in the moment and sharing their love.

"Blaze. I love you. Now, are you going to tell me why you're home so early? Not that I'm complaining, but it's not even lunchtime yet."

"Yeah, but can we have just another minute? Then we'll go to the living room. We need to talk."

"You sound so serious."

"That's because I am, Angel. I'm deadly serious."

"I don't understand, Blaze. Why do you think the rabbit was something more than just an animal kill?" Lexi sat facing him on the sofa while the dog softly snored at their feet. "There are bears and wolves, and geez, I don't know, there's probably wild boar out there, too! It could have been any number of different animals."

"You're right, it could have been. But let's think about this. You said the rabbit was pretty much shredded - bits and pieces scattered all around. If it had been an animal, they wouldn't have left that much of it behind. They would have eaten it, especially if it had been a wolf. Did you hear anything? I mean, I know you were on your Zoom call, but if there had been a large animal, you would likely have heard something. And, there was nothing else disturbed, Lexi. If it had been an animal it would have likely gotten into some other things out there, or at least tried. There are the chickens and the goats out there that are just prime for picking off. I checked, babe, there wasn't any damage to their pens and it didn't appear anything had even tried to get in. I know the possibility of this kill being caused by a human is not what you want to hear, I mean, neither do I, but looking at all the facts? I just don't see how it could have been anything but a person who left it out there."

"But why? Why would someone do that? Oh, God! Melinda? Do you think she somehow escaped prison?" Lexi grabbed ahold of his shirt in a panic.

Blaze grimaced as he thought back to the trouble they'd had with David and Melinda Osbourne and said a prayer of thanks they no longer had to deal with them. "No. No, Angel. She hasn't. I checked on that first thing this morning. She's still locked up tight and she's not going anywhere anytime soon."

"Then explain to me who and why, because I'm simply lost. I don't understand why anyone would do that."

"Lexi. There's more." Blaze filled her in on the phone calls and the cryptic message he'd received that morning.

"What? But how could anyone know something you did while you were in the special forces? I thought that was all classified and under lock and key. How could that even happen?"

"I don't know, but if that is what this is — and there's no way to be sure just yet that it is, then we need to be very, very careful. You know I dealt with and worked with some extremely dangerous people. I'm not sure how they would have gotten their hands on the files or how they would have figured out something I did that they feel is unforgivable, but I don't want to take any chances."

"So, what do we do?" Lexi scooted closer to him and then crawled in his lap, giving and offering comfort.

"Well, I was able to get enough clearance to fill Kaminski in on some of the things this might be related to. We're going to take some time tomorrow and go through the files my commander sent. Some of the information had to be redacted, of course, but there's still quite a bit that we should be able to put together. We'll see if we can make a list of potential problems and break it down from there into people who would have the highest likelihood of being involved. There are a few things that stand out to me, but the biggest, and the thing I'm most worried about, is the day that I lost Brandon."

Sadness crossed his face, a mask of pain that he could no longer hide. The day in the jungle when he'd saved the life of a little girl and, in turn, had not been there to protect his friend, had been the most horrific day of his life. Yes, he'd managed to get the girl back to her mother unharmed, but in turn, he'd watched as multiple sniper bullets pierced his friend's chest. Then he'd watched as blood seeped from the corner of his mouth, his eyes glazed over, and his life drained from his body.

It had been too much for him, and even though he'd already been on his way out of the service, it had been the final push he'd needed to run as far and as fast as he could away from the pits of hell he'd been living in for years. It had been the reason he'd returned to West Virginia and the reason that he'd been out looking for a place of his own the day that he crashed into the side of the mountain and found the woman he now held in his arms.

"Oh, Blaze! Do you really think that has something to do with this?" Worry haunted her eyes as she searched the depths of his chocolate-brown irises.

"It's a possibility I can't rule out yet, Angel. Then again, like I said, it could have absolutely nothing to do with my time in the service. It could be that I pissed off someone around here. I know I haven't been doing this job that long, but off the top of my head, I can already name at least a dozen different cases that might have riled someone up enough to be an asshole. And who knows if the rabbit and the calls are connected to each other? Maybe. Maybe not. But until we know, I need you to be careful, okay? Promise me that you'll keep Lucky with you when you go outside. And while I know that you usually only wear your tracker bracelet when we go out, I'd like for you to keep it on until we figure out what exactly is going on."

"Okay. I can do that. Promise me you'll be extra careful, too, alright?"

"I will. I just hope that I'm being paranoid and reading more into this than there is."

"Me, too."

Blaze looked down at his watch to check the time. "I need to head back to the office and put some more work in on this drug ring. The guy that we arrested yesterday is only a cog in the wheel and he didn't give up much info. I'm going to take him back into interrogation today. Hopefully, I can get something more out of him and we can continue up the chain until we close it all down."

"Okay. I'm headed back into the studio to get this song recorded." He smiled as he stood and leaned down to kiss her goodbye.

"I'll see you this evening, Angel of mine."

Lexi spent the remainder of the afternoon working on her song, perfecting the recording until it was just as she wanted. When she finally closed the door to her studio and stretched, she realized just how tense her body was. Thinking it was time for some self-care, she slowly climbed the stairs and went directly to her bathroom to fill her sunken tub. As the water flowed from the tap in a perfect cascade and began to fill the deep tub, she stripped out of her clothes, tied her hair atop her head, and dropped a bath bomb into the steamy basin.

The house had been her design, right down to the last nook and cranny. And when she'd designed the main bathroom, it had been with luxurious indulgence on her mind. Since Blaze had moved in, she'd been concerned that what had worked for her wouldn't work for him. But after many conversations, he'd convinced her that he didn't want to make changes to her design. In fact, he'd reminded her repeatedly that the first time he'd seen the house he'd wanted it. That had been the day they met, the day that had changed them both for the better.

No, the only change that he'd asked to make to the house was the addition of a television as he had a thing for movies – specifically for comedies and cult classics. She'd been agreeable and now a flat screen hung on the once-barren wall over the fireplace.

Since they'd found each other, she found it easier and easier to open herself back up to the parts of her life she'd once closed out. She'd even added a stereo system so she could have music playing throughout the house. Blaze had been the key that had unlocked the door to her music, had helped her find the music within herself again, and in doing so, had opened her heart to having music around her once more.

Before she got into the tub she walked into her bedroom, removed her tracker bracelet and earrings, and grabbed the book she was reading from her nightstand. She was halfway done with it and anxious to see what happened next in the story. Standing next to the tub, she took a look around to make sure she had what she needed, then turned off the faucet and stepped into the steamy water. Then settling back with her head pillowed on a towel, she opened her book and was immediately lost in the story that the author painted with her words.

It wasn't long before she began to nod off, so she set the book aside, leaned back, and closed her eyes. Lazily she drifted, in and out of sleep – a cat nap that made her feel as if she was floating on clouds. Eventually, she succumbed to the sleepiness that had engulfed her, content with the future that stretched before her, at last.

A half-hour later, a feeling of unease yanked Lexi out of sleep and from the beginning of a wonderful dream. She sat up with a start and looked around, confused, heart racing with alarm. When an unfamiliar sound reached her ears, she looked toward the open door of the bathroom and held her breath, not daring to make a sound as she waited to see if she heard the noise again.

A minute passed and then another, and when all remained quiet, she began to breathe easy once more.

She tried to think back. Had she locked the doors to the house? She wasn't sure. After Blaze left to return to the office, her mind had been wandering in a thousand different directions. She had stopped at one point in the afternoon to let Lucky out to potty, but she really couldn't recall if she locked the door behind them when they'd returned to the house. It simply wasn't something she was used to doing during the daytime. She sat a moment longer and when she didn't hear the noise again, she decided it was time to get out, get dressed, and get busy thinking of her safety. She stepped out of the tub, quickly dried off, and wrapped the towel tightly around her body.

She'd just stepped into their bedroom when it dawned on her that she hadn't heard anything from the dog. Surely, she thought, if there was trouble, Lucky would have alerted her. The knowledge that they'd trained the dog well made her relax further and she shook her head at herself. The conversation she'd had with Blaze had messed with her head. She dressed and then made her way downstairs to look for him and let him out once more before she began making dinner.

When she entered the living room, she saw him curled on his bed sound asleep. The sweet picture he made lying next to the fireplace made her smile. De-

ciding to let him sleep a bit more, she walked into the
kitchen to get herself a glass of wine. When she did, she
stopped cold in her tracks, fear racing down her spine in
a downward spiral of dread. Her heart began to pound
again, pumping hard in her chest and throbbing in her
ears.

The back door stood ajar and she knew without a
doubt she had closed it. She may not have locked it, but
she always made sure the doors were closed. While she
loved animals, she didn't want any wild ones wandering into the house.

She looked around in a panic but didn't see anything
out of place. Knowing she was going to have to check
the house, she reached into the drawer where she kept
her handgun and pulled it out. She checked the cham-
ber on her Smith & Wesson to make sure it was loaded,
then walked over to the door and closed it with a quiet
click, twisting the lock in place. Then having no other
choice, she began to move quietly through the house,
checking each room for an intrusion, looking under
beds, and behind furniture, and trying to take notice if
anything was missing or moved.

When she'd gone through the entire house and found
nothing amiss, she returned to the kitchen and stored
the gun once more. Breathing a sigh of relief, she called
for Lucky. When he didn't come immediately she called
again and walked toward the living room, teasing him

as she went for sleeping so hard. When again there was no response, she glanced uneasily to where he lay.

She called again, louder this time, and when she saw no movement from the dog, panic roared through her body once more, a screaming rollercoaster that made her stomach bottom out in fear.

With a scream, Lexi ran to where he lay and scooped him into her arms. Tears immediately began to flow as she tried and tried to get a response from her four-legged best friend.

"Oh, my God! Lucky! Lucky!" Then as she looked down at his chest she saw him take a breath and she felt a touch of relief settle around her shoulders. She tried her best to calm down, to see if she could tell what was wrong with him. Breathing, he was definitely breathing, but his breaths were slow and shallow.

"Okay. Vet. I have to get you to the veterinarian's office." She rose and scooped him into her arms, struggling under his weight as she hurried out the door and out to her truck. Once she had him settled, she rushed back into the house, grabbed her purse and her phone, and ran back to the truck. When the truck roared to life, she floored the gas pedal, sending gravel flying as she hurried down the twisting, winding driveway in her rush to get help.

When she made the turn out onto the mountain road, she hit a button on her phone and called Blaze to fill him in. She'd just begun to tell him everything when she rounded a curve in the road and almost slammed into a truck sitting sideways across the narrow path. She screamed as she threw on the brakes and her truck slid sideways in the loose gravel, coming to rest parallel with the truck she'd almost hit. Her body jerked with the sudden stop, her head yo-yo-ing with the movement.

With Blaze's panicked voice coming through her speakers, she threw the truck into park and inhaled deeply, looking over to where the dog lay, undisturbed by the near collision. When she assured herself Lucky was where he was supposed to be, she looked out the windshield to where the offending black truck loomed ominously.

"I'm okay, Blaze. We're okay. But there's a truck in the road." The tinted windows didn't allow her to see into the truck, but assuming the driver was injured, she released her seatbelt and pushed open her door. "The driver must be hurt. Just a minute. I'm going to go check on him." Without thinking of anything but the need to assure herself the driver was alright, and with the urgency pressing down on her to get to the veterinarian's office, she jumped out of her truck.

Her feet had just hit the roadway when a hand clamped down on her from behind, covering her mouth and nose with a cloth and jerking her back against a tall, muscular body. She began to struggle and fight but another arm encircled her, restraining her movements. She kicked, she screamed, but it wasn't long before her body began to succumb to the drugs she unwillingly inhaled into her system.

Her last thought as her eyes closed, giving up their fight to stay open, to be aware, was that she hadn't done the one thing that Blaze had asked her to do.

Her tracking bracelet. She hadn't remembered to put it back on after her bath. Now it lay on the dresser in her bedroom, a beacon of hope sounding its alarm into the void.

Unconsciousness crashed around her, a heavy curtain weighing her body down into a catacomb of darkness.

Chapter Nine

When Blaze got Lexi's call he rushed out the door to go meet her at the vet's office. He'd just pulled out of the parking lot and made the turn onto Main Street when she screamed into the phone. The frightened tone in her voice and the unusual sounds of her tires gripping for purchase on the gravel road had terrified him, causing dread to settle into the pit of his stomach.

After she'd spoken with him he managed to set aside some of his fear. But then he'd heard her get out of her truck and the sounds of a struggle had crawled through the open line of the call. Then the call went dead. Fear, as he'd never before known, grabbed his heart in a vice grip. Knowing nothing but that Lexi was in trouble, that she needed help, that the dog needed help, he floored it, flipping his lights and siren on as he blew past the town limits.

He tried repeatedly to get Lexi back on the line with no luck. Knowing time was of the essence, he made a call to the Sheriff.

Twisting and turning with the rise and fall of the land, the serpentine path seemed to take forever to travel. He drove as fast as he dared, and knowing that should he wreck he would be of no use to Lexi, he used as much caution as possible.

When at last he rounded the curve and saw her truck sitting in the middle of the road, he slammed on his brakes and slid to a stop. Lexi's black four-wheel-drive sat abandoned with the driver's side door open, a gaping maw, ominous and foreboding. Blaze jumped from his own truck in a panic and ran toward the open door, praying he was wrong.

When he got there, his worst fears were confirmed – Lexi was nowhere in sight. Her purse and phone remained in the truck along with Lucky who had begun to whimper. Looking around, Blaze began to yell her name, calling for her in case she was somewhere close by. But he knew it was of no use. She was gone.

He reached for his phone to pull up the tracking app just as the Sheriff rounded the corner and came to a stop behind his truck.

"Come on, come on, come on! Damn it!"

"What the hell happened here?"

"I don't fucking know! I'm trying to get the tracker location, but the app is buffering."

"Son, I'm going to need you to calm down. Take a breath and walk me through what you know."

By the time Blaze had filled him in, the app finally connected and opened to reveal the location of the tracker.

"Shit, shit! Okay. Here we go. What the? Oh, God. Oh, fuck!"

"What?"

"It says she's at the house. She's not there. There's no way she would leave Lucky. That means she wasn't fucking wearing the bracelet when she left the house. Fuck. And that means we have no idea where she's been taken."

The hopefulness that had been coursing through Blaze as he raced up the mountain, drained from his body in a slow crawl. Stoney-faced and resolute, ice formed in his veins, and the happy, sarcastic joker who had appeared more than two years ago, vanished in a heartbeat. All that remained now was the hardened shell of the special ops soldier, the military specialist - deadly and frightening. His eyes, once so full of warmth, life, and love, now held nothing more than a dark void. His once smiling mouth, graced with an endearing crooked lift at one corner, was now set in a hard line. His entire persona had been replaced with a resolve of steel.

He was a lethal weapon ready and waiting to be deployed. He would get Lexi back. Somehow. Some way. He was determined to get her back in his arms and never let go.

Sheriff Kaminski saw the change come over Blaze and knew he had a ticking timebomb on his hands. Invisible warning flags waved in the air around the soldier who now stood before him with the words "handle with care" emblazoned on the banners.

He'd known bits and pieces of the hell Blaze had endured in the military, but now, thanks to the files that had been delivered to their office that morning, he had a much deeper understanding. And he knew that until they had Lexi back, safe and sound, there would be no return of the friend and co-worker he'd gotten to know so well.

"Soldier," the Sheriff cautiously stepped closer to him, coming eye-to-eye with the killer who stood before him, "we need to get a plan in place. First things first, I'm going to call someone to come take care of getting Lucky some care. Are you okay with that? My wife can be here quickly and she'll take him to the vet. I need you to answer me yes or no, son. Nobody is touching that dog until you understand that he will be properly seen to by caring hands. Have I made myself clear? Do you understand?"

"Yes, Sheriff. I understand. Call her. It will be one less worry on my mind right now."

"Alright." Stephen cautiously stepped back and placed the call. Warily, he watched Blaze as he began searching the area surrounding Lexi's truck. Then, assured that his wife was on the way and she understood the direness of the situation, he began searching, as well.

Eventually, they both came back to the truck empty-handed. Lexi had vanished without a trace. Blaze opened the passenger side door and began to carefully examine the dog. When dark eyes opened, blinked briefly as they tried to focus, and then closed once more, Blaze nodded his head.

"I may be wrong, but I think they slipped him something to knock him out. I'm going to feel better if he's examined, but I think he's going to be fine. God, Lexi must have been out of her mind when she realized she couldn't get Lucky to wake up."

"I'm sure she was."

"How do you want to handle this?"

"I want to call in the search team. Let's map out the area, and divide it into quadrants. We start on the roads and go off-road and on foot when and if we find something. I doubt there's going to be anything on the truck, but we'll dust it anyway. It will probably be the same story at your house, but we'll dust there, too. Chances are, whoever has her never touched the truck, and likely had on gloves when they were at the house. But we cover our bases and follow the book, alright?" Cautiously, he watched Blaze's behavior and inwardly grimaced. He knew that was one powder keg he did not want to set off.

"Yeah. I got it."

The sound of an engine reached their ears before it rounded the bend in the road and came to rest behind the Sheriff's truck – a caboose at the end of their train of vehicles now taking up the roadway. Stephen watched as his wife climbed quickly from her car and rushed to where they stood. Sandra immediately made to go to Blaze to offer comfort, but her husband stopped her and cautioned her with a look of trepidation. Wary of Blaze's mindset, she went to him and spoke gently as she engulfed him in a hug.

"Blaze. I'm sorry. Don't you worry about Lucky. I've got him. One of you just put him in my backseat and I'll be on my way. I'll take really good care of him, alright? Y'all just get our girl back."

"Thanks, Sandra. I'll move him over." Blaze went to Lexi's truck and hefted the dog in his arms to transfer him to the other vehicle.

"How's he doing?" She looked up at her husband and he could see the worry she had for their friends written all over her face.

"Tick, tick, tick."

"That's what I was afraid of. She has to be alright, Stephen. She just has to be." She turned to her husband and hugged him once more before hurrying back to the waiting dog. Finding a wide spot in the road, she carefully maneuvered her car and headed back down the mountain.

Stephen looked to where Blaze stood, military stiffness in his stance as he awaited orders. The blank look that had settled in Blaze's features was disheartening. Taking a deep breath and squaring his shoulders, Stephen took command of the operation.

"Alright, Deputy. There's a fingerprint kit in my truck. You get it and dust the truck. I'll call the search team. Let's get this party started."

Lexi's head throbbed in agony, a pounding bass drum that boomed with each heartbeat all the way across her forehead and in a line straight down the middle of her skull. Her eyelids were heavy and though she managed to open them a few times, so far she'd been unable to keep them open for any length of time. Her body felt logy; her muscles were weighed down by an invisible force. She had no strength to lift a finger and though she tried repeatedly, she didn't manage to move at all. She tried calling out, calling for Blaze, but only managed a whimper.

Time lost all meaning as consciousness played peek-a-boo with her brain. In and out of awareness she went, sleeping then waking in a repeating pattern. And while her body fought off whatever drug she'd been given, her heart ached for the man she loved. She prayed that he could feel her heart reaching out to his, and she prayed that he found her soon.

Thoughts of the anguish and terror he must be feeling twisted and turned inside her, churning in an angry sea of remorse with each minute that passed. She was sorry she'd questioned him. She was sorry she hadn't been more cautious. And most of all, she was sorry he was hurting in any way.

Her body tired quickly from the struggle to stay awake and eventually, it simply gave out. Succumbing to the lingering effects of the drugs once more, she closed her eyes and let the heaviness take her under.

Two hours later Blaze and Lexi's home had been transformed into a central headquarters. They organized as quickly as possible. Maps of the area were divided and teams of two formed – one driver, one lookout, to try and cover as much ground as possible before the sun went down. Each vehicle carried emergency kits and each kit was outfitted with first aid needs, flares, thermal space blankets, and portable spotlights.

Blaze watched as each team left the house and began winding their way down the driveway and out to their assigned sectors. He'd worked with most of the team members before. It wasn't unusual for them to have people go missing – hikers unfamiliar with the area who manage to get themselves lost, people who wander off the marked trails and are unable to find their way back. And though he'd worked with the team and had faith in them and their abilities, he couldn't help but be apprehensive.

He wouldn't, he couldn't, lose Lexi. She was his best friend and lover, his soulmate, and happy ever after. She was the air that allowed him to breathe, the blood that pumped through his body. She was the balm to his past, the ambrosia of his present, and the nirvana to his future.

She was his. Plain and simple.

He'd already reached out to some friends of his own and called in the last of the markers on favors he was owed. The men he contacted were exactly like him — smart, observant, calculating, determined, and deadly as fuck. He'd served with them and fought next to them at various points in his military career. They shared a bond that a civilian would never, could never, understand. The men he called had immediately headed to the airport. Even as Blaze started the engine of his truck and took off down the driveway to begin searching his own area, his friends were in the air and rushing to his aid.

He trusted them with his life, but more importantly, he trusted them with Lexi's.

Taking a right at the end of the drive, Blaze, who had been teamed up with a local paramedic, began twisting and winding his way down the mountain. When he rounded the first bend in the road and came upon the very spot where he'd wrecked his truck, the spot where he'd come face to face with his destiny, he felt the anger that he'd been controlling with a very tight leash, slowly beginning to shred the tether that bound it.

Whoever had taken her was going to regret their decision. And, he thought, God help them if she was found with even the tiniest scratch on her radiant skin. With steely-eyed determination, Blaze gathered his thoughts and made a solemn vow: harming Lexi in any way at all would be a death sentence for her captor. He didn't care that he now wore a badge. The long arm of the law could only do so much. Her captor was going to pay – one way or another.

Fifteen miles away Lexi's kidnapper rode along in companionable silence. No music played on the radio and the only sounds that made it to his ears were the sounds of the engine revving as it climbed yet another incline through the mountain pass, and the occasional question from the driver as they determined which direction to go with each junction they encountered. He made a show of concentrating on the road, the trees, and the mountainside, looking for all intents and purposes as if he was truly trying to find some sign of Lexi and where she might have been taken.

It had been pitifully easy to blend in with the search and rescue team. He'd been in the area long enough now that the locals were familiar and friendly with him. Now he was partnered with one of the Sheriff's Deputies and was playing the role of a concerned citizen. He'd enjoyed the pain underneath the surface of the controlled rage that Blaze tried so hard to hide.

He'd stood around the outer edge of the group of searchers, hiding his face as best he could to avoid any kind of recognition from Blaze. As he lurked, he noticed each nuance of anguish that had flashed in the man's eyes. He preened with each tiny crack of Blaze's voice as emotions he tried to tamp down snuck through his bravado. Others might not have noticed, but he did. He'd been studying Blaze for a while. He'd watched and learned.

Blaze was the sole reason that his own life would never recover, and would never be as it once was. He felt he'd had no other choice but to learn all he could of the man who had stolen from him, the man who had taken all that mattered from him.

Months and months of research and digging had finally paid off. But when he'd gotten his hands on the missing information, it had taken many more months of researching and digging to find out where Blaze had disappeared to.

He considered himself fortunate when one of the search parameters he'd scheduled to run non-stop had dinged on an article from the local newspaper in an out-of-the-way tiny dot on the map. That article had not only found him the man he'd been hunting but had given him the focus for his revenge.

Lexi Lane.

Thinking of the woman he currently had drugged and tied up, he craned his neck to look out the window so he could hide the smile on his face. He felt certain he had her in the one location nobody would think to look. Or, at least they wouldn't until it was too late.

He'd been watching her for a while. He studied her comings and goings and discovered a pattern in her daily routine. The rabbit had been a warning, an omen of things to come. But instead of her screaming "eek" and calling Blaze to come to her rescue, she'd cleaned up the mess herself. He knew then that he wasn't dealing with any ordinary woman. She had balls of steel and knowing that she was not only smart, but resourceful, strong, and gutsy, he'd shifted his original plan. Lexi wasn't a woman to play the part of a damsel in distress and he hadn't fully prepared for that possibility.

As she'd buried the rabbit remains at the edge of the property, he'd quietly disappeared into the wooded acreage and rethought his plan.

He'd tried to mess with Blaze a little bit, too, pulling a mind-fuck by leaving hangups on his voicemail. He'd known the calls wouldn't be anything Blaze would worry about — at least not until he decided to leave his cryptic message. And though his message had screamed bad teenage horror movie, he thought it had been effective.

Part of his plan revision had been the addition of drugging the dog. He hadn't seen the canine show anything but a fun and loving demeanor until the discovery of the rabbit. That was when he knew he was going to have to subdue him in some way to be able to get to Lexi.

He'd also known that getting Lexi out of the house and away from any weapons they might own was going to increase his success rate in taking her away from Blaze. Yes, he thought, so far his plan revisions had worked in his favor and everything was falling into place.

Soon, very soon, Blaze was going to feel the same pain he felt and experience the same impotent rage that coursed through his own body daily.

Michael Blaisure was going to lose it all. He would accept nothing less than the complete and utter destruction of the man who had taken away everything he'd ever cared about.

It was time for Blaze to pay for his sins.

Chapter Ten

Lexi's body ached. She was stiff and sore from lack of movement. She had no idea how much time had passed, but as she blinked a few times, she found she was finally able to open her eyes and keep them open. What she saw made her stomach churn with dread. The sun had begun to set. The lone window she could see out of showed the darkening shadows of twilight. She'd been missing for hours.

Quickly, before she completely lost the light of day, she looked more closely at her surroundings. She knew immediately where she'd been taken and a glimmer of hope began to form inside her heart.

She was in one of the cabins at the camp.

One of the completed cabins, as it smelled of fresh paint and newly laid flooring. She was restrained on the railing of one of the four bunk beds, and her body rested on one of the three-inch thick foam paddings that the campers would spread their sleeping bags upon.

Twisting from her side to her back to try to get some relief from the pressure points she'd been lying on, she came face to face with a note from her captor. Attached with duct tape to the bottom of the bunk bed atop hers and written in black marker, the note simply said, "Don't worry. I'm coming back for you."

Lexi shivered. How, she wondered, could a note sound hopeful yet ominous at the same time?

The warmth of the spring day was fading fast and though she was in an enclosure, the temperature was beginning to dip. She saw no blankets, nothing to cover herself with as she peered at her surroundings. And even if she'd found one, she knew there was no way she could have gotten to it to spread it across herself. The leather straps of her restraints gave her no wiggle room to reach more than a couple of inches from the railing.

Even though she knew it was useless, she struggled against the straps in hopes they would loosen and she could free herself.

She tried to think back, to remember exactly what happened and how she'd gotten into the cabin, but the memories were blurry and faded quickly up to the point they became non-existent. She remembered finding the back door ajar and the panic setting in upon its discovery. She remembered finding Lucky unconscious and trying to rush him to find help. And she vaguely remembered stopping for a truck stalled in the road. Other than that, she was clueless.

Her mind began to race with questions and horrific scenarios. And though she tried not to go down a dark path, she found that was the only direction her thoughts seemed to want to travel. The harder she tried to be positive, the worse the negative thoughts intruded. Finally, she gave up and tried to escape into sleep once more.

It didn't take long until she began to drift, but even as she drifted her mind continued to work overtime. She knew all she could do was wait to see who her kidnapper was and why they'd taken her. And she knew all she could do while she waited was hope and pray that Blaze found her quickly.

Night had fallen and the first stars had begun to appear in the clear, dark sky. They glittered in the darkness and filled Blaze with a touch of hope for Lexi's safe return. He had dropped his search partner off back at the house with her vow for a fresh start early the next morning. And though Blaze knew he needed to get some rest, he simply couldn't. There would be no rest for him until Lexi was in his arms once more.

Thanks to Sandra Kaminski and her help in getting Lucky to the vet, he now knew the dog was alright. He'd been heavily drugged, but the veterinarian didn't foresee any issues, no long-term effects. That, at least, was one worry off his mind.

Many of the other searchers had called it a night, as well, but a few had decided to stick it out and try to cover more ground. Alone he drove through the mountains hoping for some sign of Lexi's whereabouts, and as he drove he thought back over every moment of their relationship.

Images of the first time they'd met flashed through his mind in rapid succession. The late winter snowstorm that seemed to come from nowhere, then waking in her living room to the warmth and glow of the fireplace. She'd been so reserved, so brave, and as much as his body had felt an instant physical attraction, it had been the connection they'd made heart to heart and soul to soul that had told him their meeting had been kismet.

He pictured her in the kitchen as she washed dishes, chasing a soap bubble as it floated upon the air until she popped it with her finger. The laugh that followed made him grin with happiness.

He could see her as she worked in her flower garden and tended to the goats and chickens. Pride in herself for what she'd built on her little plot of land beamed in her smile.

He could sense her all around him. He could hear her rich alto voice as she sang. He could smell the fragrant bouquet of her skin — an aroma that was hers and hers alone. He could feel the silkiness of her smooth skin as his roughened hands traced each curve, peak, and valley. He could taste the honeyed sweetness that pooled between her legs for him when she came, the liquid warmth always making him hunger for more.

He was afraid. Part of him didn't want to admit that because it had been ingrained in him from an early age that admitting you're afraid isn't manly, and showing fear isn't something that tough, manly men do. But he knew, thanks to Lexi and thanks to his therapy sessions, that being able to acknowledge your fears and face them is the only way to deal with and move past them.

He stared out into the night as the spotlights atop his truck illuminated a wide swath for his field of vision. There has to be something, he thought. There has to be some sign of her somewhere. He couldn't bear to think otherwise.

He reached for the cold cup of coffee in his console and gulped down the last of the bitter brew in hopes of giving himself a caffeine boost. As he swallowed heavily, he blinked back unshed tears and continued searching.

The door to the cabin burst open with enough force that it bounced off the freshly painted wall and as it did, a deep male voice echoed in greeting.

"Honey! I'm home!"

Lexi's heart raced as her eyes flew open. She immediately regretted it and squeezed them shut once more when she was blinded by the glare of the flashlight shining in her face.

"Time to get up! Sorry it took me so long to get back to you. I had quite a bit of work to do before I could return. You know...you're a hard woman to find. Or, at least that's what I've led the rest of the search team to believe. You're not too uncomfortable, are you? I mean, I've been inside your house. I saw your playroom. One or both of you enjoy being tied up while you have a little hanky spanky fun and I'm fairly certain that it's you."

The voice of her captor was familiar even though there was something off about it. Lexi blinked against the harsh light once again. She hoped her eyes would begin to cooperate so she might be able to see enough to figure out his identity. But when she finally became accustomed to the single light bouncing around the room with his movements, she still couldn't see enough of him to figure it out.

"Who are you? What do you want with me?"

"Oh, we'll get to that. Right now, I've got some food for ya – part of the reason it took me so long to get back – and I'm sure you need a bathroom break. Ya know, I'm glad the camp has come as far as it has so quickly. I can't turn the light on as that might draw attention to the cabin, but at least there's a working toilet." Her captor walked to her then and began loosening her ties. "Now, before you get any bright ideas in that smart little head of yours, let me just shoot them down now." When Lexi heard the click of the safety and felt the cool metal of a gun against her skin, she stilled instantly. "If you try anything, and I do mean anything at all, then our fun and games will end before they've even started. Do you understand, beautiful?"

When Lexi didn't immediately respond he became irritated.

"Answer me," he growled.

"Yes. Yes, I understand." Though Lexi tried to remain strong, her voice trembled in fear.

"That's more like it." He finished untying the leather straps and grabbing her by the arm, jerked her off the bed. "Now, the bathroom door stays open, and here," he reached into a brown paper bag she hadn't been aware he'd brought in with him and pulled out a stack of napkins, "this will have to do. If it looks like this is going to take a while, I'll make sure to get a roll of toilet paper. Hell, I'll even splurge for the good stuff. Everyone should have a few luxuries for their last days on earth."

Lexi took the stack with her and quickly made her way into the bathroom to relieve herself. She'd just walked out again when he shoved the paper bag at her.

"Another part of the reason it took me so long to get back to you. By the time I finally got away from the search party, got in town, grabbed you a burger, and got it back up here... Well, it took a while. It's probably cold, but it's food."

She sat on the side of the bed and unwrapped her dinner. Cold? Yes. But it was a Ma's burger which was good no matter what, and it would give her the sustenance she was going to need to survive whatever he had planned for her. She took a bite and chewed slowly, hoping he would continue to talk to her and shed some light on what the hell was going on.

"Now. I'm going to answer your questions, although I have to tell you that I'm hurt, deeply hurt that you haven't recognized me yet."

There was something in the tone of his voice that finally began to ring a bell with her, and when he tilted the flashlight toward himself, he confirmed her thoughts.

Bradley Hayden. Stunned, she could do nothing but stare. Why had her new construction site foreman taken her and what did he want?

When she finally managed to speak again, all she could manage was a single word. "Why?"

"Well now, that's the big question and the answer might surprise you. Let me begin by telling you a story." Lexi took another bite of the burger and listened intently as he sat down on the bed across from her and began to tell her why he'd taken her and what he intended to do. "Once upon a time, there were two brothers - twins to be exact. They went everywhere together and did everything together. They were inseparable. Or, they were right up until they graduated high school.

"You see, it was then that one brother made the decision to go to college, while the other brother joined the military. The brother who went to college studied hard, earned an architecture degree, and went on to build a business for himself, designing and drawing up plans for homes and businesses. The brother who joined the military was successful as well, and quickly gained rank and title.

"The brothers spoke almost every day, even if it was nothing more than a quick text to check in with each other. For years they lived like this until one day those texts stopped coming regularly. You see, it was at that point that the brother in the military became a member of a covert military group. He was no longer allowed to have easy access to communication devices. On the rare occasions that he managed to call or text his brother, he wasn't able to share where he was or what he was doing.

"But the one thing he did share was that he had a friend, a best friend, and they looked out for each other. And though his brother worried still, it eased his mind to know that someone had his brother's back.

"Then one day word came that the brother in the military had been killed in action. The remaining brother was devastated. In his despair, he simply stopped living. No amount of sympathy or empathy could break through his pain and give him a reason to carry on with his life. Day in and day out he suffered silently, locking himself in his home, in his bedroom, and worst of all, locking himself in the memories of the past. He couldn't pull himself from the abyss and move forward with his life."

He stopped in his storytelling at that point, laid the gun beside him on the bed, and pulled a flask from his back pocket. He unscrewed the cap and took a few deep pulls from the silver canteen and screwed the cap back on as he swallowed.

"So, you're the brother?"

"Now, now. Don't get ahead of me." He switched out the flask for the gun and gripping the weapon in both hands, began again. "The architect brother had someone special in his life. They were in love. They had been together for about a year when the brother was killed. The lover understood that it was going to take time for healing to begin and was very patient with the brother. The lover offered to take the brother to therapy, even offered to pay for it, but the brother couldn't even get himself out of bed to do daily activities, much less something as monumental as leaving the house, getting in a car, and going to sit in a therapists office.

"The lover reached out to several therapists and tried to schedule telehealth therapy. But still, the brother refused, preferring to barely exist rather than seek help. He hardly ate, he hardly drank, and he rarely bothered to get out of bed. The lover watched the brother slowly begin to fade away. His physical health declined almost as rapidly as his mental health. His skin, once youthful and taut, began to sag and his bones, once well-protected by layers of muscle, became prominent and jutted from his body unnaturally. His hair, once thick and silky, began to fall out in clumps. His eyes, once vibrant and full of happiness, became dark and lifeless.

"The brother withered away right before his lover's eyes." Once more Bradley switched out the gun for the flask and drank deeply before continuing with his story.

"His lover finally reached a point where they could no longer live their life under those conditions. But, instead of packing their things and leaving, moving on with their life, they decided they couldn't live without the brother. And in their mind, the brother was just as dead as the one who'd been killed in combat." Lexi felt tears begin to sting her eyes. She knew what was coming and it broke her heart. "On a sweltering hot summer day, the lover walked into their garage and started both of their cars. With the garage doors down and sealed tight, the lover lay on the floor between the cars and let the fumes pull the life from their body.

"Yes, Lexi. I am the brother." Lexi's eyes shifted to the gun lying next to his leg. Seeing her looking at the gun, he grimaced and shook his head to discourage her. "There's more to this story, but I see the direction your thoughts have taken and I really don't have it in me to fight you right now. So if you're done eating, I'll tie you up again. Behave and I'll finish my story."

Feeling she had no other choice, Lexi shifted and laid down, allowing him to restrain her once more.

"Now, where was I? Oh, yes. So, my lover killed himself because I couldn't get my shit together. Losing him was a wake-up call. I lost my brother. I lost my lover. And I eventually realized that I'd lost myself. When I finally came out of my mental lockdown, I decided that I needed to know why. What happened the day Brandon was killed? Where was he? What was going on? Who was with him? And more importantly, where was this so-called friend who always had his back?

"There was only so much information given to my family. To find out the truth, I had to take matters into my own hands. It took time. It took money. And it took entering the dark web and finding hackers to give me the answers I sought.

"Ah, yes. I can see from the look on your face that you know at least some of those answers. Once I finally knew the truth, I knew what I had to do. It took me a while longer to track down Blaze. I have to hand it to him, he knows how to vanish when he wants to. The moment the scale tipped in my favor was when you were attacked. Your story came out then and when it did, Blaze's name became linked with yours.

"I finally had my answers and I finally found the man responsible. At that point, I had no idea what to do with the information, or the best way to get my revenge. So I waited, biding my time as I tried to formulate a plan. Then, the announcement came about the camp, about your involvement. It was as if a gateway opened, and after contemplating the best way to achieve my goal, a plan popped into my head. Blaze allowed the person who meant the most to me in this world to die. And because my brother died, I lost myself and I lost my lover. At that moment it became my goal to take from him just as he had taken from me. I want him to suffer as I have suffered. I want him to know that he is the reason for his own anguish.

"Michael "Blaze" Blaisure is going to feel the pain I've felt for the rest of his life."

Chapter Eleven

Blaze pressed on the brake and put his truck into park, bowing his head in defeat. He needed food. He needed rest. He needed Lexi.

He'd driven for hours and had, in fact, driven so much that he had to make a trip to get more gas so he could continue driving in the morning. He'd made sure that his cell phone was on full volume and fully charged, but he knew there were pockets where cell service was spotty. He'd relied on the police radio in his truck, too, but as of yet, no word had come with news of her location. Eventually, exhaustion began to overwhelm him and it hadn't taken long for him to decide to return and try to re-fuel his body.

Now, he was home. As he looked up at the windows of the A-frame and saw the glowing lights shining from within, he knew he wasn't ready to walk inside. Just the thought that Lexi wouldn't be there waiting for him with open arms was enough to make him want to hurl. But knowing that there were other people there invading their space while manning the command center for her search party made him want to commit murder.

They were necessary and he knew that, but it didn't stop him from wanting to throw everyone out of the house in impotent rage.

He refused to believe she was gone without a trace. There had to be something somewhere that would lead them to her location. He wondered if whoever had taken her would eventually reach out with some kind of demand. Everything seemed so orchestrated. There has to be more to it, he thought, than just abducting Lexi. If it truly had to do with him and his time in the military, he was certain of a few things: One – This was going to get ugly. Two – Whoever had her would eventually try to leverage her for whatever they were truly after. And three – Lexi was in grave danger. He didn't know what he would do if she were ever harmed, or, God forbid, if she became a fatality.

Scrubbing his gritty, tired eyes, he leaned his head back against the headrest of his truck. He needed a moment to gather himself before he walked into the house and looked into the concerned faces of his friends and co-workers. He needed a moment to get his head on straight before he walked into the powder keg of memories that awaited him in every nook and cranny of the home he and Lexi shared.

He closed his eyes and slowly counted backward from ten - one of the coping mechanisms he'd learned to utilize when he started going to therapy. He thought of each number as a problem or an irritant he was letting go of to reduce his feelings of being overwhelmed. The further he counted down, the less splintered his mind became so that he could concentrate on one or two things instead of the multitude of variables that often seemed to bombard his critical thinking capabilities.

The next thing he became aware of was someone calling his name. Startled, he jerked awake and began to look around, alert and ready for action, his hand automatically reaching for the gun he wore holstered on his hip. When he realized that it was the Sheriff, he relaxed and exited his truck.

"Anything?"

"No. You were the last one out. Everyone else has checked in and headed home for the night. We've still got Ms. Eliza and another volunteer inside, but I think they are both about to pack up, too. Everyone's set to come back at daybreak and get a fresh start."

"That's good. I figure everyone needs some food and sleep."

"You definitely look like you could use some. Ms. Eliza brought in dinner for everyone and she's got a plate heating up for ya. Why don't you come on in and see if you can get some fuel in ya?"

"Yeah, I'm headed that way." Blaze looked at the house with trepidation. He wasn't certain how he was going to make it through the night without her by his side. It would be one thing if she was away on a trip, but not knowing where she was or how she was doing was making him lose his mind.

"We're going to find her, son."

Blaze nodded his head and slowly began the walk up the stairs and into the house, bracing himself for the onslaught of memories and emotions headed his way.

In the dim light afforded by the flashlight, Lexi saw Bradley glance over to where she lay confined to the bed. Part of her wanted to feel sorry for the man before her, and part of her wanted to kick his ass before Blaze threw him in jail.

"There's not much more to the story. Once I knew what I was going to do, and where I was going to go, all that was left was to figure out the best way to accomplish my mission. It was easy enough to get on the construction crew for the camp. I've been here for months. I've studied you. I've studied Blaze. I know your habits, your likes, your dislikes.

"When the site foreman decided to retire it was the opening I needed. My architectural background and work ethic were big green check marks with the construction company. When they appointed me to replace him, I was able to move up my timeline and adjust my plans. I now have full access to the camp and nobody questions my coming or going – no matter the time of day or night. Having several of the cabins completely finished and furnished, gave me the perfect location to put you while I carry out the rest of my retribution. There's no reason for anyone to be in the completed cabins now so the chances of you being discovered are next to zero."

"What are you going to do with me?"

"For now? Keep you here. Eventually, you'll have to die. But not before I observe Blaze in as much anguish as possible. Now, I need to get some rest and just in case I don't get up here before the crew tomorrow, I'm going to have to keep you quiet."

He walked to her then and placed a ball gag in her mouth, securing it around her head. "I figured you wouldn't mind this. I mean, it came from your own dirty little stash. Nice room by the way. And I guess you're used to being tied up so nothing new here. You're in luck, though. I did bring a blanket with me. I mean, I'm not completely heartless. If circumstances had been different, I think you and I would have gotten along nicely. Love your music, by the way."

He grabbed the blanket she hadn't seen him carry in and spread it across her body.

"Sleep well."

And with that, he walked out the door and left her in the dark. The tears came quickly and Lexi once again began to pray that Blaze could hear her heart calling out to him through the night.

Blaze found himself wandering through the house and down to the music room in the middle of the night. Sleep simply would not come. After tossing and turning for what seemed like forever, he gave up and made his way downstairs. The heaviness in his heart weighed down his body and his sluggish movements were exaggerated as he let despair take over. Now he sat on her piano stool and lightly ran his fingers over the ebony and ivory keys.

With one finger he began to pick out a tune that Lexi had tried to show him, but failed. He didn't have the ear for music or the talent that radiated from every pore of her body. Looking around the room, he studied each instrument and piece of equipment she used in her work. Then seeing her painting easel in the corner with a drape-covered canvas on it, he got curious.

He went to it and raised the thin material, letting it drop to the floor as he stared at her colorful creation. When they first met she'd been unable to tap into her musical side so she had let her creativity out through painting. Her pieces had been dark, angry, and full of hurt, anguish, and desperation. Once she'd unlocked the door to the music within, she'd set her painting aside, preferring to return to the roots of her creative soul.

Evidently, she'd recently picked it up again as the piece that he found was one he'd never seen before. But where her pieces before had been dark and full of rage, this one was overflowing with light, happiness, and love. It was a physical representation of where she was in life, of the love in her heart, of the love between the two of them. When Blaze realized what he was looking at, he dropped to his knees and screamed his frustrations, his worries, and his rage and anguish at having the love of his life taken from him.

He finally released his feelings, unwound the band of strength and hope he'd been clinging to, and let the shattered pieces of his heart fall before him.

Once he had purged himself, he got to his feet and stumbled wearily up the stairs and back to bed. Even though his nightmares were rare now, he knew as soon as his head hit the pillow and his mind began to shut down that one was coming. It was going to be bad, and there was nothing he could do about it. Exhaustion quickly took him under and almost immediately the horror began.

Hand-in-hand they strolled across a sandy beach as the sun shone brightly down upon the thin slip of land. Tall cliffs towered over them in the background and an aura of days gone by echoed in the salty sea air. They wore white, just as they'd done in a prior version of this particular nightmare. The rich blue of the sky, the deep teal green of the ocean, and the dark brown of the wet sand contrasted vividly with the dark stone of the cliffs and made their white clothing stand out brilliantly. Gulls called, swooping and circling for food. Masses of tiny shorebirds ran back and forth with the undulating tide.

Lost in love he gathered her close. His crooked grin spread as a glint in his eye flashed. She looked up at him, her vividly green eyes alight with love, laughter, and happiness. Ur-

gently he claimed her mouth, his ache for her overwhelming, and she met him, need for need. The kiss deepened as hunger spread, consuming him from within, and all sense of time vanished as they explored.

It's the same, he thought, exactly the same as before. He sighed with happiness even as a warning tingle of awareness began to crawl from his neck down his spine. As intrepid thoughts of disaster slowly crept into his mind, a feeling of dread began to bloom in his chest.

Caught up in their explorations, neither noticed the brilliance of the sun as it began to dim and the dark storm clouds that rolled in to hover ominously over their heads. The first raindrops began to fall, an occasional plop of wetness that tickled with each scattered bead. The wind, absent when they first stepped onto the beach, began to swirl around them, increasing in intensity moment by moment. They looked up in confusion at the ever-darkening sky.

Soon it was as if a vortex had opened around them and the storm began to rage. They broke apart and even though the wind began to gust and the black clouds began to pour, Lexi merely laughed as she glanced around.

The ocean waves, so calm before the storm, now tossed and turned, rolling angrily against the shore. Their crests grew higher and crashed down harder as the storm began to release its fury upon them.

He knew they needed shelter and as he too anxiously looked around, he spotted a small structure nestled against the cliffs where a brilliant light shone like a homing beacon. He grabbed her by the hand once more and yelled over the thunderous storm. "Run!"

His legs pumped hard and his feet pounded against the dark sand as he pulled Lexi along. They ran hard, but the sand swallowed their footsteps and the harder they ran, the further they seemed to sink. Soon the shifting sand reached his knees and he stumbled with every step. He began to tire and his lungs began to burn as they struggled against the forces of nature. It wasn't enough. He wasn't fast enough. He wasn't strong enough. He wasn't brave enough.

He wasn't enough.

When he once again looked back at Lexi, he froze in fear. Stark horror at what he saw made his heart stop beating.

Black ocean waves dominated the background, hovering over them as if they had been waiting for Blaze to turn and see their ominous forbearance. And when they knew they had Blaze's attention, slammed down upon the shoreline behind Lexi. Thunder boomed and the earth beneath Lexi's feet crumbled. As her face froze in horror, she let go of Blaze's hand and disappeared into the depths of the rolling sea.

He raced to the edge and dove in after her. He held his breath as he swam and dove, swam and dove. It was pitch black as he searched and he could feel the force of the waves as they continued to barrel down upon the once-calm waters of the ocean. With each powerful stroke of his arms, he reached and grabbed in hopes of latching on to her. Each time he came up empty-handed. His lungs caught fire as he continued to hold his breath, and the lack of oxygen began to compress his chest - and still he searched. His heart, pounding hard with fear when he entered the water, began to slow to a thready staccato beat as the last of his breath began to leave his body.

He'd failed. Lexi was gone. He had no reason to carry on.

Floating as the ocean whirled angrily around him, he gave in to despair. With his final thoughts on his love for Lexi, he closed his eyes and opened his mouth to swallow the salty ocean water that would send him to his final resting place...

Surging out of the nightmare, Blaze jackknifed off the mattress. Gasping for breath, lungs on fire, burning just as they had in the dream, his eyes raced around their bedroom. Home. He was home, but Lexi was gone.

Sweat poured off his forehead and beaded across his tattooed and scarred chest as he sucked in deep lungfuls of air to try and quench the searing fire that scorched his lungs. As the nightmare came back to him and played on a loop in his mind, he buried his head in his hands and tried to clear his head.

He couldn't break down. There was no time. Lexi needed him and he would accept nothing less than a clear mind, a rested body, and his unparalleled instincts and skill. He was getting Lexi back. He was going to hold her in his arms again.

He was finding her and he was doing it today.

Steeling himself for what lay ahead of him, he crawled out of bed and made his way to the shower to cleanse the cold, clammy sweat from his skin.

The last drop of freshly brewed coffee fell into the glass carafe just as a loud knock on the front door echoed throughout the house. It was just barely daylight, but as he'd been unable to go back to sleep, he'd gone ahead and gotten ready for the day. Blaze poured the dark steaming liquid into his coffee mug and replaced the carafe on the burner. Taking a sip, he went to answer the door and was unsurprised to see the Sheriff and Ms. Eliza waiting on the other side. The aroma from the warming trays they carried hit his nose and made his stomach rumble with hunger – a reminder that he needed to eat to have the energy he would need for the day ahead.

"Blaze."

"Morning, Sheriff. Ms. Eliza."

Ms. Eliza barreled through the door, a force of nature in her own right, and headed straight to the kitchen. "Got breakfast sandwiches ready for everyone – enough to feed a small army. We gotta make sure and send everyone out with full bellies. It's going to be a long day."

Blaze and the Sheriff looked at each other and grinned as they followed after her. "I appreciate that Ms. Eliza."

"Oh now, it wasn't any trouble at all. You just concentrate on getting our Lexi back and I'll make sure you're well-fed until she is."

"That's my plan – getting her back. I'm getting her back today. I'm not going to stop until she's back here where she belongs."

Setting the tray he carried on the kitchen island, the Sheriff lifted the foil and offered a sandwich to Blaze as he grabbed one for himself. "Any thoughts on how to make that happen, son?"

"Not a clue. I do think it would be a good idea to swap out sectors, though. Maybe someone will catch something someone else missed yesterday."

The sound of a loud engine carried through the house as the first of the volunteers began to arrive.

"Alright. Let's get the crew fed, and the assignments made, and then let's get to it. We shouldn't waste any daylight if we can help it."

Blaze heard the front door open and the thud of heavy boots as help began to pour into the house. Recognizing their gait, he grinned and was unsurprised when he looked up to see his friends Tank and Viper leading a small group of volunteers as they walked into the kitchen. He greeted his friends with a hard, bone-crushing hug and thanked them for coming.

"Thank fuck you're here!"

"No need to thank us. Markers be damned, Blaze. Lexi is yours – that makes her ours." Tank looked toward where Viper stood and nodded his head for confirmation.

"Agreed," Viper added. "We got you and we're going to get her back."

Thankfulness flooded Blaze, a tidal wave of relief. Now, he thought, it's time to get my angel back.

Chapter Twelve

T hirty minutes later Blaze stood next to the Sheriff and Deputy Shaver on the front deck of the house as he addressed the assembled group of searchers crowded around for their briefing.

"Ladies and gentlemen, you've got your partners and assignments. I want check-ins every half-hour. Tell me where you are and what you see. Even if it seems inconsequential, I want to know about it. Switch off your driving every hour and give yourself a different view, give the driver a break. Most of all," he looked up at the overcast sky, "keep an eye on this weather. There's a major storm headed our way and it has the potential to be catastrophic. Ms. Eliza and her sister are here keeping tabs with the National Weather Service and they will update you with the latest as it approaches or if anything changes. You all have lived in these mountains much longer than I have, but I know as well as you do that when these severe storms hit, they can be disastrous. Roads wash out and flash flooding can happen in these valleys in the blink of an eye. Mud and rock slides can start in an instant. Do not, and I repeat this, do not drive through any flooded areas. Turn around, go back, and loop around. Don't get yourself washed down the mountain. We don't need to have our attention divided because we're having to perform a secondary search and rescue."

He took a moment to look through the crowd to drive home his point and when he received nods of understanding, he dismissed them. "Alright, let's do this."

Deputy Shaver joined his partner as the others dispersed. Two by two they paired off, a ragtag group of volunteers anxious to begin their searches. As car doors began to echo, engines roared to life and the searchers began to wind their way down the drive, the Sheriff turned to look at Blaze. "Are you sure you don't want me to go with you? Everyone has a partner except you."

"Not for long." Blaze nodded toward the driveway and called the Sheriff's attention to the car going against the grain of exiting vehicles. The Sheriff grinned when he saw his wife park her car. When she opened the door, Lucky jumped across her lap and landed on the ground with a thud before bolting up the deck stairs and straight into Blaze's waiting arms. "There you are. Hey big guy! How ya doin'?" Blaze gave Lucky all of his attention for a moment and Lucky returned the love with happy barks and excited licks of affection.

Looking up at the Sheriff as he greeted the dog, he continued, "Not that I don't trust Ms. Eliza and her sister, but I would feel better having you here at the base coordinating everything. You might see something, some pattern as the reports come in. I trust your instincts. So, yes, I'm sure. Besides, I'll have this big guy with me, and he's just the partner I want right now."

"Then that's the way we'll do it."

Blaze rose then and jogged down the steps to his truck, calling for Lucky as he went. "Blaze," the Sheriff called out, "we're going to get her back."

Opening his truck door, Blaze looked up to where he stood and nodded in agreement as Lucky leaped inside. "You're damn right we are."

Ten minutes later Blaze parked beside the four-wheel drive that his friends had rented and hopped out of the truck, Lucky on his heels. He'd sent a text to his friends while the Sheriff had been giving his speech back at the house, quickly choosing a spot and time to meet up once everyone had been dismissed.

"Did you see him?" Blaze looked hopefully back and forth between his friends.

"Tall, lean, full dark brown beard. Kept the brim of his cap down low so you really had to look closely to see his eyes. Stayed just on the edge of the searchers. Lurking and watching." Tank looked over to where Viper stood nodding his head in agreement. "Yeah. We saw him, Blaze. We also saw him sneak off when he thought nobody was looking. He must have had a car tucked away somewhere close by."

"Yeah, that's what I was thinking. It's him. I know it's him." Blaze shook his head in disbelief. "He searched with us yesterday. He fucking joined the search party for the woman he abducted. That takes balls."

"That or he's just fucking stupid," Viper added.

"There's something familiar about him..." Blaze trailed off. "I can't put my finger on it, but I could almost swear I know this guy."

"Someone from around here?"

"No. Or, at least I don't think so." Blaze reached into his pocket and grabbed his phone. "I'm going to check in with the Sheriff and see if we can figure out anything about him. I was concentrating so damn hard on the fact that Lexi had been taken that I wasn't paying as much attention as I should have to who all showed up for the search party. If we can figure out who he is, or who he claims to be, maybe we can get a better idea about where he ran off to. And with any fucking luck," Blaze looked up from the keyboard on his phone to meet the hardened eyes of his friends, "we can get a damn clue as to where he's taken my Angel."

"Maybe we should have left those cameras up in your yard after all that shit with the Osbournes went down." Viper shook his head in disgust.

"I can tell you this, my friend, those bitches are going to be reinstalled as soon as I can get to it. I can't go through something like this again." Blaze met their gazes with steely determination.

Though the morning sun was shining, a rumble of thunder broke through the atmosphere. The three men looked to the heavens with trepidation.

"Fuck. I hate it when there's thunder and the sun is this bright. In my experience, it means there's some bad shit headed this way." Tank pulled out his phone and brought up a weather map. "Shit. It's going to get really bad, real quick. We better figure out what we're doing and get moving."

Blaze looked up from his phone, a new raging fire burning in his eyes. "Kaminski asked around. He says that this guy is the damn foreman at Lexi's camp."

"You're kidding."

"Nope. And guess what else? Lexi told me that he fucking hit on her recently."

"Okay. We need someone to check the place he's rented and someone to go to the camp. Maybe some of the crew can give us some more details on the son of a bitch," Viper chimed in.

"Yeah. How about you guys take the rental and I'll hit the camp? A bunch of the crew joined the search party, but if there's anyone there today, they might be more willing to talk to me instead of two jacked-up guys they've never seen before."

Blaze's phone pinged again and he quickly looked at the message, "Thank you, Sheriff! Here," Blaze sent his friends a copy of the text, "this is where he's been staying." He looked back and forth between his friends. "You know what to do."

Lexi's body hurt. She was stiff and sore from being restrained to the bed. Her jaw ached from the constant pressure of the ball gag, and her throat was dry because of the difficulty swallowing. And to top it all off, she desperately had to pee again. The pain and pressure in her stomach had been building for the past hour or so and was now at the point of agony. She was determined not to piss herself, but if Bradley didn't return soon, she knew she was going to have no other choice. The thought of doing that and then having to lay in it until he decided to show back up made her sick to her stomach.

She'd fallen asleep the night before with tears streaming down her face and now her eyes hurt, as well, puffy and swollen. Her head hurt, too, the pain throbbing in time with her heartbeats. The painful remnants of her crying jag made her feel as if she was in hangover hell.

The sun had begun to rise a few minutes earlier and as it had, the darkness of the cabin started to fade. She was thankful to be able to see her surroundings but at the same time, it was a dismal reminder of her situation.

She'd tried to keep her wits about her after he left the night before and not completely lose it as despair threatened to overwhelm her. As she lay there waiting for sleep to claim her, she'd begun to formulate a plan. Now, she ran through those thoughts again to try to prepare herself for whatever came her way throughout the day.

She knew there were three ways she could get out of this mess. Blaze could come barging through the door and rescue her. One of the construction workers could happen to find her. Or, she could dig deep and gather every bit of courage, strength, and quick-thinking abilities she possessed and outsmart and hopefully overpower her captor.

She hoped and prayed for option number one but would settle for option number two. But if it came down to it, she knew that she would fight tooth and nail to make option number three a reality. Her survival instincts were strong – had always been strong - and now that she had Blaze in her life, they'd gotten even stronger.

No matter how long or hard she had to fight, she wasn't going down without giving her all to stay alive and return to Blaze and the life they'd planned together.

As more pressure built in her bladder, Lexi tried to think of other things to take her mind off her need to use the bathroom. Thinking of music seemed to help and soon she found herself working on a new song. She'd just started to work out a chord progression for the chorus when she heard the first of the construction crew begin to arrive on site. Hope bloomed within and she began to kick against the wall of the cabin in hopes that the worker might hear and come to investigate.

When the door to the cabin burst open and slammed into the wall behind it, she knew she'd fucked up. Her eyes darted quickly to where Bradley stood, his large frame filling the doorway while menacing anger rolled off him like a thick fog. Fear skated down her spine, a cold slithering menace that left her quaking, dreading whatever punishment he was about to dole out. He stormed to the bed and backhanded her across her cheek, muttering curses at her as he did. Her head snapped to the side with the force of the impact. Her teeth jarred and pain seared as she involuntarily bit down on the hard rubber of the ball gag.

Overwhelmed, tears sprang to her eyes as she tried to catch her breath. Her stomach began to roil and her gag reflex began to kick in. Her body heaved as she tried her hardest to hold down the bile that threatened to choke her. When he reached for her again, she winced, but when he ripped the ball gag from her mouth, she was finally able to suck in deep lungfuls of air. When he struck her again, she gave in to the tears and let them fall as his heated words berated her and her failed attempt at discovery.

"Did you actually think anyone was going to hear you? They're not due at the site for a while! Want to know why? Because their understanding and super helpful site foreman gave them a couple of hours off to go help with the search for their favorite missing musician! Wasn't that nice of me?" He began tearing at her bindings and when she was free, jerked her up and off the mattress pad. When she was on her feet he gave her a forceful shove toward the bathroom and threw more napkins at her. "Do your business quickly so I can get back out there and join the search. I've got to make it look good, right?"

Lexi quickly relieved herself, grateful that the pressure in her abdomen could finally begin to ease. She swiped at the tears and rubbed her tender jaw. Not only was she hurting from the altercation, but her jaw had developed an ache from the weird position she'd had to maintain due to the ball gag.

When she walked back into the room gently massaging her wrists, he shoved a foil-wrapped sandwich into her hands. "Compliments of Ms.Eliza. Enjoy. It's likely to be your last meal because I have a feeling today will be the day I confront Blaze."

Lexi began unwrapping the sandwich, warily keeping an eye on him as he continued. "I can't wait. I'm going to make certain that he knows the anguish, that he feels the despair that I feel. I had thought about killing him, too. But I decided he needs to live. You see, I may not come out of this alive, but neither will you. He needs to live with the agony of knowing that you're gone and that it's all his fucking fault. I wonder...do you think he will just kill himself or live with the pain? One way or another he will end up in hell where he belongs."

The sun that had been shining so brightly began to fade as he spoke and the cabin slowly took on the shadows produced by the cloud cover of a stormy day. Lexi looked around as she ate the breakfast sandwich he'd brought. She chewed slowly trying her hardest to pro-long their encounter as she searched for something she could use as a weapon. And as she ate and searched, the first fat raindrops began to ping off the metal roof of the cabin.

Tank and Viper looked at each other, hints of "oh fuck" written on their faces.

After Blaze informed the Sheriff of his suspicions, multiple phone calls had been made and through the legal magic of an emergency search warrant, Tank and Viper were duly authorized to enter Bradley's residence to look for anything that might point them in the direction of Lexi and why she'd been taken.

It had been ridiculously easy for them to get into the ramshackle single-wide trailer located at the address Blaze had sent them. There wasn't much inside the tin can of a shelter. A sleeper sofa sat in the living room, the bed extended with a lone pillow and meticulously straightened sheets. A cardboard box served as a make-shift dresser, neatly folded clothing the only contents. A small round clothes basket sat beside it with a single day's dirty clothes awaiting the wash.

Nothing decorated the walls. No television sat waiting to be watched. The only other furniture item in the entire residence was a lone backless wooden stool that sat next to a spotless countertop in the kitchen. A microwave, a toaster, and a laptop sat on the countertop and a quick search of the cabinets revealed a single plate and plastic cup, one fork, knife, and spoon. There were no pots and pans and the only food to be found was a loaf of bread, peanut butter and jelly, and a couple of takeout containers in an otherwise pristine fridge.

The bathroom had revealed the bare minimum, as well, and told them nothing about the man they suspected had taken Lexi.

It wasn't until Viper turned on the laptop that their suspicions were confirmed. Password protected, he frowned at the screen and tried using "Lexi" as the code. When that failed, he shrugged his shoulders and typed "Blaze" into the prompt. The screen came to life and a single folder appeared on the desktop – "Blaze Will Pay." He opened the folder and began going through the files, while Tank read over his shoulder.

"Son of a bitch..." Tank grabbed his phone and quickly dialed Blaze to tell him what they'd found.

Blaze parked his truck at the top of the hill which looked down onto the camp and glanced around in confusion. Several work trucks and construction vehicles sat in the makeshift parking area, but there was nobody to be seen. The lack of construction noise and movement immediately made him leary. He knew quite a few of the construction crew had volunteered to help with the search, but he'd expected to find at least some of the crew arriving for work by that time. His intuition began to buzz and warning bells began to ring loudly in his ears.

The wind had picked up and quick-moving clouds darkened the day. He stepped from the truck and Lucky bounded after him as the swirling sky broke loose and the rain that had been falling in spurts and spatters, rapidly turned into an angry downpour.

He looked up at the sky and cursing to himself, began to slowly and warily make his way down to the site while Lucky trotted along next to him. And as he neared the first building, his phone began to buzz in the cup holder of his truck console and the screen lit up with an incoming call from Tank.

"Shit! He isn't answering!"

"Keep trying. I'm calling Kaminski. He needs to see this – the sooner, the better."

"Agreed"

Viper pulled up the Sheriff's number and as soon as he answered, began quickly filling him in on everything they had found.

"It's bad, Sheriff. He somehow has gotten his hands on all kinds of sealed records. It all dates back about five years. And there are links to articles about Lexi, the camp -there are even articles about everything they went through with David and Melinda. There's stuff about Lexi before she left Nashville and there's tons of documents on Blaze's Black Ops missions over the past few years."

"Son of a bitch. Where's Blaze? He hasn't checked in."

"Last we talked to him he was headed to the camp to see if he could get any of the workers to tell him about this foreman. We tried calling but he isn't picking up."

"Damn it. Okay. Don't touch anything else. One of you stay there in case this asshole comes back, and one of you go meet me at the site. And be careful! This storm is getting crazy out there."

"On it!" Viper ended the call and looked at Tank who just shook his head. Blaze still wasn't answering his phone.

"I'll go, Tank. You stay here and wait for the Sheriff."

With a fist bump of agreement, Viper rushed out the door.

Chapter Thirteen

The pounding of the rain on the roof of the cabin was deafening as the storm grew in intensity. The wind howled and the sky thundered.

"Now then. It's time for me to go and see if I can find you somewhere. Assume the position."

Lexi looked up into the dark eyes of her captor and finding nothing but emptiness there, knew there was to be no consoling conversation, no amount of reasoning, that would get through to him. When Bradley lost his brother and his lover, he'd subsequently lost himself and any sense of understanding and humanity that he'd ever possessed. Though she knew it was pointless, she felt she had to keep trying anyway.

"Please don't do this."

"I thought you were made of sterner stuff than this?" He began walking toward her with the restraints. "Please don't beg, Lexi. You know it won't work."

He reached for her wrist and as he did, Lexi decided it was time to show him just exactly what she was made of. He began to loop the restraint around her wrist, and knowing he wouldn't expect it, she jerked the cord to bring his head closer to her and headbutted him at the same time as she balled her other hand into a fist and punched him in the stomach. It took every bit of strength she had, but surprising him worked to her advantage. As he lunged for her, she quickly brought her knee up under his chin and snapped his head back one more time.

She didn't waste any time as she saw him trying to recover from the stun of her hits, and she jumped up and raced toward the door. She burst through to the driving rain of the storm as she tried her best to escape. She ran as quickly as she could, but she wasn't fast enough as her feet lost traction on the soggy ground. She wasn't far from the cabin door when she felt herself being tackled into the muddy terrain. Air whooshed from her lungs as her body absorbed the hit and she landed with an oompf. Immediately, the weight of her captor pressed down on her as he thwarted her attempt by sitting on her back. She could hear him yelling at her, but it wasn't until he grabbed her by the hair and

slammed her face into the ground that his words started breaking through the thunderous noise of the storm.

"You stupid bitch!"

She winced in pain and opened her mouth to try to
take in air, to try to scream, but her lungs didn't seem
to want to cooperate. When she finally managed to suck
in enough of a breath to relieve the burning in her chest,
she felt him wrench her head back once more.

"Stupid, stupid, bitch! I should just kill you now!"

As she fought and struggled against his hold, Lexi
closed her eyes and prayed as hard as she could that
someone would come to her rescue.

Blaze found himself going from building to building at the construction site battling sheets of rain. The
gravel laid as a temporary drive to the site quickly began to wash away, and muddy streams littered with
silt and gravel ran swiftly across the property. He could
hear Lucky whining loudly next to him as he cautiously
searched through the cabins and main structures. Each
time he cleared a building and came out empty-handed,
he felt a bit more defeated.

Even without confirmation, he knew without a doubt he was the reason Lexi had been taken. Somehow, some way, he was going to figure out who and why. And when he did, he thought, whoever was behind her abduction was going to pay dearly.

He'd just come out of the dining hall and started across to the remaining cabins when a blur of movement caught his eye. His stomach plunged and his heart raced as the horror of the scene before him began to unfold in gruesome detail. Unparalleled rage stole his breath and years of training for mental and physical warfare surged through his body. In an instant, he became the predator. A monster. A killing machine with no off switch.

His body was in motion before he fully registered that he was moving. Legs pumping and arms swinging as he raced across the property, Blaze was a lethal bullet and Lexi's captor was a bullseye. The wildness of the storm as it thundered and poured covered the sounds of his approach until it was too late for the target to do more than look up in surprise when Blaze yelled. He let go of Lexi mere seconds before Blaze dove and tackled him, dislodging his body from atop Lexi's. Together they rolled and when they finally stopped, a crimson haze clouded Blaze's vision.

He began to punch and pummel the man on the ground beneath him and the man fought back. Bones crunched as fists flew. Curses and death threats were hurled at each other. And when Blaze landed a well-placed fist against the man's jaw and a tooth came flying out of his mouth, Blaze's smile was filled with satisfaction.

He could feel the man's strength begin to wane, but he kept going and with one final punch, knocked the man out. Chest heaving with exertion, Blaze withdrew his SOG SEAL Strike knife from the nylon sheath on his belt. It was black, lethal, and a perfect fit in his tattooed hands. Blind rage coursed through his veins and clouded his vision as he gave in to the unbridled need to protect his woman and punish the evil that had tried to destroy them. With the hilt in two hands and arms raised above his head, he prepared to strike.

The abject terror in Lexi's scream broke through his hazy vision and stopped his downward motion.

"No! Blaze! Don't! Don't kill him! Blaze!"

He looked down to see the man lying beneath him, unmoving and mouth agape as bruises began to slowly form across his face. He shook his head to try to clear the fog, to find his way back from the edge. And when Lexi called to him once more, he looked over to where she waited, Lucky at her side – guard dog on duty.

"Michael! Please! Come back to me!"

Realizing that he'd almost crossed the line, he dropped his arms and relaxed his shoulders, letting his head fall back and the rain wash away the crimson that stained his vision. He re-sheathed his knife and quickly scrambled over to her on his hands and knees. His need to get to her, to hold her was an all-consuming fire, erasing all other thoughts from his mind. When he reached her, he grabbed and pulled her close. Enfolding her in his powerful arms, he held on tightly while she trembled against his chest.

Lexi's body was an earthquake of emotions as she shook with terror. "Oh God! I've got you, Angel! I've got you!"

"Don't let go, Blaze."

"You're safe now. You're safe."

And while the skies continued to rage, Blaze claimed her mouth. His lips pressed against hers and when she opened for him, he dove for more, succumbing to his need to reassure himself that she was truly in his arms, to reassure her that she was safe. Give and take, take and give, they fed from each other until they completely lost track of where they were and how much time had passed.

When at last they came up for air, a low growl and angry bark rang of warning. Startled, they glanced over to see her abductor running, stumbling in his haste, into the woods, and down one of the mountain paths.

"Damn it! I didn't cuff him!"

"Go. Don't let him get away, Blaze."

"Here." He reached into his pocket and withdrew his keys. "My truck is at the top of the hill. You're freezing. Go. Take Lucky with you. Get warm and call for help. He won't get far."

"Come back to me. Don't let the rage take you over again, okay? I need you. I need the man I love to come back to me."

"I will. I'll always come back to you, Lexi."

He kissed her quickly and then was up and running full-tilt after her abductor.

"Blaze! It's about damn time you checked in!"

"Sheriff, it's me. I'm at the site. I'm okay but Blaze has gone after Bradley on his own."

Lexi sat in Blaze's truck with the heater going full blast. She and Lucky were soaked through and making a mess all over the truck, but she was very thankful to be away from Bradley and away from the cabin. Now, she thought, we just have to get Blaze back up here and make this son of a bitch pay.

"Lexi! Thank God! It's damn good to hear your voice! We've been trying to reach him. We figured out who had you but not where. Alright, I'm on my way. Stay there. Do not try to go after him."

"No worries. Lucky and I are quite content and not too proud to say we're glad we have a knight in shining armor out there defending us."

She heard a car door slam and an engine start.

"We'll be there as soon as we can."

"We?"

"Yeah. We. Blaze called in Viper and Tank. One of them should be at the site soon and I'm not far behind."

"I should have known he'd bring his guys in."

"You should know by now that man will do anything for you. See you soon!"

Lexi hung up the phone and hugged Lucky close to her side. "Help is on the way, big guy."

Lucky gave a happy yip and licked her cheek. Suddenly the past couple of days came crashing down on her and when she thought of all she'd been through and the relief she felt that her ordeal was almost over, she buried her face in the dog's fur and let herself cry. Sometimes, she thought, the best way to deal with an overload of emotions was to let them pour from your soul.

Blaze ran on instinct, trying his hardest to hear and see over and through the deluge that continued to fall from the sky. The path, barely there to begin with, was made treacherous by the continuing storm. Strong gusts of wind whipped through the trees causing branches to strike out as he passed, stinging his skin with the force of their slaps. The snap-back cap he perpetually wore offered him the barest minimum of protection from the water cascading around him, and the shit-kicker boots he wore, while heavy on his feet, allowed him some stability as he maneuvered through the uneven landscape and hurtled over small bushes and fallen trees.

His prey was fast, but he was faster. It wasn't long before a flash of movement just ahead of him caught his attention. Blaze felt the urgency to capture his quarry rise from deep within himself. He pushed his body to its limits, using every ounce of strength, speed, and agility he owned.

Lexi's captor suddenly stopped and turned, bracing himself for the attack coming his way. Blaze once again launched himself at the man and they began to roll, grappling for purchase against the downward slope of the mountain as they fought.

Blaze knew they weren't far from the edge of a deep ravine, and as they tumbled he searched for some way to stop their fall. He reached and grabbed over and over until his hand landed on the hard wood of a small tree. Catching himself and stopping his descent, his body jerked and his arm wrenched from the force of the sudden stop dislodging himself from his opponent.

His actions slowed the other man's descent and Blaze watched as he tumbled a few more feet before coming to rest mere inches from the cliff's edge. Blaze heaved a sigh of relief when the man didn't disappear over the rim, and he watched as he slowly rose to his hands and knees.

Hate-filled but familiar eyes stared up at him and in an instant Blaze was taken back.

Mission after mission, through some of the most stressful and challenging times in his life, he'd seen those same eyes. They'd never been filled with hate, though – only friendship and trust. His heart, already beating madly from the chase, began to pound hard enough that he thought it would burst through his chest. No, he thought, it couldn't be.

"Brandon?" The name slipped from his lips in disbelief and confusion.

"No, mother fucker." The response was snarled at him and filled with just as much hate as his eyes. "I'm his brother. His twin brother."

"Oh, God! Bradley. You're Bradley."

A loud clap of thunder had Blaze looking to the sky with concern, and when he looked back, it was just in time to see the ledge that Bradley was lying on begin to crumble and fall. Blaze reached for him, but it was too late. Wide-eyed with fear and terror, Bradley dropped out of sight in an instant.

More and more of the ledge began to fall and Blaze, realizing he was in danger, rolled and began to rapidly crawl his way up the steep, slippery incline. When at last he was able to stand, he turned and looked back down to the edge of the cliff.

Heartbroken, confused, and desperately needing to feel the woman he loved in his arms, he began the long hike back to the site – back to Lexi.

Blaze's mind raced as he trudged his way back up the mountain and through the dense forest. And as he hiked back to the site, the storm gradually began to ease. Flashes of the past began to weigh down on him and thoughts and feelings about his friend's death came rushing back to be front and center in his mind.

He and Brandon had been the best of friends – they'd been family. And though Brandon had shared stories about his brother, Blaze had never put it together that they were twins. The beard had thrown him, but once he'd gotten a look into Bradley's eyes, it had been obvious. Laying there clinging to a tree to keep from being too close to the edge of the mountain, his past had come roaring back at him like a pouncing lion, landing on his chest and stealing his breath.

He'd spent months and months after Brandon's death going over the incident, each and every moment, every step he'd taken. He'd spent hours upon hours wondering if he could have done something, changed something - if doing or not doing one thing or another would have brought a different outcome in whether his friend lived or died. And every night he'd revisited that hell in a never-ending nightmare that played on repeat. Those horrific scenes would play out in his mind and he would wake up screaming in agony, covered in sweat and heart racing. It had been a living hell.

Then he'd met Lexi.

Lexi was his lifeboat, his anchor. Falling for her had been the push he'd needed to seek help. Leaving her sleeping in her bed and walking away after their first meeting had eaten away at his heart. He'd known he needed to be able to offer her the world, and he'd known it would never be possible until he could safely say that his own heart and mind were, at the very least, on the mend.

Picking up the phone and making his first therapy appointment had been a struggle, but the day that he'd walked into the therapist's office had been another huge turning point in his life. It was then that his world had begun to right itself, and when he'd reunited with Lexi, everything had fallen perfectly into place.

Now, not only had he lost Brandon, but he'd failed his friend once again by letting his brother die. The chances of his survival after the ledge gave way into the ravine were minuscule. Bradley had acted in retaliation for Brandon's death, for Blaze's part in the death, however inadvertently, and that revenge had almost cost him Lexi.

As all the nightmares of the past danced before his eyes, he wanted to scream his outrage. And as he broke through the last of the dense forest and into the cleared land of the construction site, that's just what he did.

Falling to his knees in agony, he raised his face to the sky and screamed. His chest heaved and pain engulfed him as deeply buried rage began to pour from his soul. And while he released his hurt and sorrow, the last of the storm passed and the lingering rain fell softly upon his face, washing away the tears that had finally broken free.

When at last the screaming stopped, he sat back and let the tears continue to flow. Then, feeling a familiar hand on his shoulder, he looked up into the loving eyes of the woman who held his heart.

Needing to feel her in his arms, he pulled her down into his lap and burying his face against her, held on tightly.

He'd always been told that time would heal all wounds. Now, he knew better. There was truly only one thing that could heal the heart and soul.

Love.

Chapter Fourteen

C lean and warm, Lexi and Blaze sat on the sofa, curled together as a fire burned brightly in the fireplace to knock the chill off the dreary day. The search for Lexi had been called off and the search for Bradley's body had begun.

No longer in need of a command center, everyone had dispersed with the exception of the Sheriff, Tank, and Viper. Lexi shared the story she'd been told and by the end of it, Blaze was up and pacing the living room floor.

"How did he get past Lucky?"

"I've had quite a bit of time to think about that, Blaze. Lucky was with me the last time I visited the site. Lucky was familiar with his scent. I'm sure that's how he was able to get close enough to give him whatever drug he used." Blaze continued to pace.

"You aren't responsible for his actions, son." Sheriff Kaminski watched as Blaze let everything Lexi said sink in.

"Rationally? Yes, I know that. But there is an irrational part of me that says every bit of this is my fault, going all the way back to that day in the jungle."

"You did what you thought was best at the moment. For the record, I happen to agree with that decision." Lexi turned to Blaze and held her hand out to him to offer comfort. "I know you're feeling guilty that I was taken, but the path that Bradley went down was his own choice. You can't control other people's actions any more than you can control their reactions."

"Anyone who has served has had to make hard and fast decisions at one point or another." Tank looked over to Viper who nodded his head in agreement. "Some of us more than others. We were put into some horrendous situations. It was our job, our duty. You know as well as I do that sometimes you don't have time to think, you just have to act. You have to rely heavily on your instincts. It's those split-second decisions that kept us alive, helped us take down corrupt governments, and saved the lives of innocent people. We knew what we were signing on for, and so did Brandon."

"I know. Logically, I know. I just wish there was some way I could have saved them all." Pain, deep and heartfelt, flashed in his eyes as he looked down at Lexi. "Most of all, I wish there had been some way to avoid getting you involved in all of this, of keeping you from getting hurt."

"I'm alright. I have scrapes and bruises, but I'll heal. And knowing you'll be by my side as I do brings me comfort."

"Let me ask you something." Blaze turned to the Sheriff and waited for him to continue. "Did you do your absolute best? Did you give everything you had to try to make an untenable situation better?"

"Yes, sir."

"Then that's all you can ask of yourself and you need to accept that and allow yourself some grace." Blaze blew out a rough breath and ran his hand over his beard as he contemplated the Sheriff's words.

"His family needs to know he's gone. God. I can't even imagine what their parents are going to be going through. They've lost both of their children now. I'll take care of it first thing in the morning."

"No. You won't. You're too close to this."

"But..."

"No." Sheriff Kaminski cut him off. "I'll take care of this and you're not to go near it. And that, Deputy, is an order."

"When the phone call cut off the other day, my whole damn world came crashing down around me. All I could think was that I'd lost you. Every time I imagined you being held somewhere, possibly hurt or worse, rage tore through me. It was a jagged knife carving my heart from my chest. The thought of never holding you again, of never seeing the love in your beautiful green eyes, or never hearing your voice again, absolutely shredded me. I can't imagine my life without you in it. You're my light, my hope, my salvation. Without you, the world is a dark, empty void."

With the soft glow of candlelight scattered throughout the room, Blaze and Lexi stood next to the bay window in their bedroom, his arms wrapped around her from behind, and his chin tucked into the cradle of her neck. The last of the overcast storm had cleared just before the sun was due to set and now the sky was bathed in deep amber, orange, pinks, and reds – a golden hour vision full of warmth and promise as the day began to turn to night.

"It was my fault. I wasn't careful enough."

"Don't. Don't blame yourself. You got dragged into a situation that has absolutely nothing to do with you other than your connection to me. I need to know you're alright. I see the bruises on your face and wrists, the little cuts here and there. I know those will heal. But will your heart and mind? It's weighing on me that you were hurt because of my actions. It's weighing on me that you were exposed to any kind of trauma because of my past."

"Michael. I'm alright. I'm going to be alright. I have you and you are everything that completes me and makes this world make sense. We can get through anything together."

"I don't know how I got so lucky as to find you. I don't want to ever experience this kind of fear again. You're my world."

"Can we put it aside for now? I don't want to think about Bradley anymore tonight."

"Alright. How about we take our minds off it the old-fashioned way? Are you feeling up to it?" Blaze turned his head and slowly licked a line from the base of her neck up to her ear before taking her earlobe in his mouth and sucking gently.

"I can't imagine me ever not feeling up to making love with you."

"Just one more way you bring music to my ears, Angel. Now, tell me this. Have you ever heard the old adage, "Red sky at night, sailor's delight; Red sky in morning, sailor's warning?"

Lexi giggled softly. "I have and we definitely have a red sky out there tonight."

"And you, Angel, are this sailor's delight."

"Mmm. I think you twisted that phrase for your own purposes, but this is definitely the kind of distraction I need."

"I aim to please."

Pressing his growing erection into the small of her back, he continued nuzzling her neck as he smoothed his hands up and down the silky material of the robe covering her arms. She leaned into him, soaking up his strength, and let her body relax into the tenderness of the moment. His hand drifted to her waist and slowly untied the belt holding the two halves of her robe together. As the material parted, he reached inside and trailed his fingertips softly up her body. Stomach to sternum he teased, and when he grasped the edges of the silk, he bared her naked body as he slowly eased it from her shoulders. Goosebumps of anticipation rippled up her arms and sent a shockwave of arousal straight to her core.

"Blaze... I want it all tonight. I need it all tonight. Gentle and loving, rough and ravenous. Take me. Break me. Shatter us both and then mold us back together with flames so intense they ignite our souls."

"Angel. The depths of hell are a cool breeze compared to the inferno burning inside me for you."

Touching her with nothing but his tongue, he began to lick a dewy line down her spine. Tortuously slow, he tickled and taunted as he drew the line and when he reached the hollow of her back, he paused, reveling in the softness of her skin. And then he dipped lower, maneuvering his body to the carpeted floor as he went, and sitting on his knees.

"Spread your legs, Angel."

With a shuddering breath, Lexi widened her stance. Soft kisses rained down on her ass cheeks and her body began to tremble. The nip he gave her was quick, sharp, and thrilling as his teeth bit one cheek and then the other. She gasped and gave a yelp of surprise only to have him place a hand at the small of her back and bend her over.

"Grab the edge of the window seat and hold on. Don't let go until I tell you to."

She braced herself for the onslaught of sensations she knew were headed her way. When she felt nothing but his hot breath as he teased her pussy, her dusky pink nipples peaked, tightening into hard pebbles.

"Look at you, all wet, glistening in the candlelight. I can see your arousal beginning to trickle down your legs. Mmm... I know what I want. I know what you want. But I want to hear you say it, Lexi."

Grabbing her ass cheeks, he kneaded them as he waited for her answer. With each flex of his strong hands, he revealed more and more of her and her pussy throbbed with need.

"Lick me."

"Is that all you want? A single lick?"

"No. Lick and suck me."

"And?"

"Oh, God."

"I'm waiting."

"Tease me."

His hands became more insistent, his voice going deeper and rumbling in his chest. "Angel..."

With a moan, she exhaled sharply. "No." Her voice began to quaver. "More. I need more."

"Then stop playing around and tell me, Lexi. Tell me exactly what you want, what you need." He smacked both ass cheeks to get her attention and then went back to kneading.

"Oh shit! Devour me! Fucking devour me, Blaze!"

The animalistic growl that tore from his body as he dove face-first into her exposed pussy echoed around the room, reverberating in the stillness of the night. Gasping for air as he feasted, her body shuddered and she tightened her hold on the hard edge of the window seat.

His masterful tongue worked her hard, diving deep inside before teasing his way to her clit. The protruding nub quivered as he lapped against it and within seconds they both could feel the frenzied arrival of her peak. Like a lightning bolt streaking through a darkened night sky, her orgasm flashed through her body. The searing wave of pleasure stole her breath and stars bloomed behind her eyelids, a sea of glittering diamonds flickering in time with the throbbing nerves of her clit.

Blaze broke the connection long enough to give her fair warning, "I'm not nearly done with you." Then he went back for more.

"Oh, fuck..." Lexi could hardly hold herself upright as he tortured her body with pleasure. As her legs began to give, her strength waning quickly, Blaze hooked her thighs over his shoulders and stood, arms around her waist as he continued to feast. Lexi softly yelped as she registered the sudden change in her orientation and her eyes flew open in surprise.

And still, he didn't stop.

As the blood began to rush to her head, Lexi held on tightly to his waist. Her heart rate began to slow, gradually descending from the height of her orgasm, and her mind began to clear. When she could think somewhat clearly, she realized that the rigid length of his cock waited beneath the soft, gray material of his sweatpants. She grinned wickedly and began to lower the waistband.

Springing free from its confines, his cock bobbed in anticipation. She wasted no time licking up the glistening droplet of pre-cum that waited at the tip, and then she took him fully into her hot mouth. With long, smooth strokes she sucked him in, taking him as deeply as she could before slowly inching her way back up the shaft. The soft pad of her tongue lapped at the velvety skin, tracing the thick lines of the veins pumping blood through his steely erection.

Their bodies strained as they pleasured each other and when Blaze began to feel his own orgasm rocketing through his body, he slapped a hand against the wall, a brace to hold himself upright. Raising his head and gasping for air, he rode the sensations. With each burst of cum, he grunted his pleasure, and when he felt Lexi swallowing after each surge, he once again buried his face. Moving his head back and forth, he coated his beard in her wetness, gathering a fine sheen of orgasmic glaze.

His explosion only proved to drive his need for more of her, and when the last bit of cum left his body, he walked to the bed to lay her down. With her spread out before him and her lips still wrapped around his cock, he began to pump himself into her. When he hit the back of her throat he moaned, pleasure rippling through his body. Her hands reached over her head and then behind, gripping his ass as he pumped. When he tried to back off, she held on tight, her nails digging in and scoring his ass cheeks with half-moons.

Once more he pumped and then with a growl of impatience he moaned, "Fuck, yes! You're taking my cock down so fucking far, Angel. But I need to fuck your pussy now. I need to feel myself buried deeply inside you."

With a last silky slide up the length of him as he pulled out of her mouth, Lexi gave the tip a final swirl and kiss. Then, with a grin, she rose to her knees and wrapped her arms around his neck. "What position do you want me in?"

Blaze grinned back at her, "All of them." Then he dove for her and with Lexi's squeal of delight, they landed on the mattress. He began to worship her body, laving each taut nipple with his tongue, sucking and teasing, and she watched him. The more she watched him loving her body, the more turned on she became, her hips gyrating between his body and the mattress.

When he suddenly stopped and stared into her eyes, Lexi worried that something was wrong. Then she felt him slowly begin to enter her. Inch by glorious inch he filled her, drawing out the moment. And just when she thought he was simply going to drive her mad with his teasing, he surged inside her as hard as he could. Her walls clenched around him and they moaned simultaneously as they were overcome with ecstasy.

His lips ravished hers as he poured himself into the kiss, and she simply melted. Her muscles, taut with anticipation, liquified and she looped her arms around his neck to draw him closer. Licking inside her mouth, tongue battling against tongue, he overpowered her with his hunger and she let herself be taken. Whatever he needed, whatever he wanted – all he had to do was take and enjoy. Then without breaking the kiss, he began to move, and with every thrust of his hips, he mimicked the move against her mouth. When Lexi's hips began to move with him, meeting him thrust for thrust, they both lost what tiny bit of sanity they'd been holding onto.

Arms and legs tangled together as they rolled from one side of the bed to the other. When Blaze was once again on top of her, he grabbed her legs and pulled them up, spreading her into a wide vee.

"Grab your ankles, Angel. Open up and let me watch my cock slide into you."

And as she did, the guttural moans that came from him turned her insides to jelly.

"That's it. Fuck... Look how we fit together. You were made for me, Lexi. That's it, Angel. Take all of my cock."

Lexi's eyes began to roll back in her head as she felt her next orgasm clawing its way from the depths of her core. She gasped for breath as Blaze continued to impale her.

"Oh, I think you're going to come again. Your clit is getting so swollen. Touch yourself. I want to see you play with your clit. Make yourself come around my cock. I want to feel your pussy clamp so hard around me that I can hardly move to fuck you."

Biting her bottom lip, she grinned at him and held up two fingers to his mouth for him to wet. He licked and sucked them, coating them in his saliva, flicking his tongue against them briefly before releasing them. And then she reached between her legs and gathered more of the wetness from her first orgasm before circling her clit.

"That's it. Fuck I love to see you play with yourself. More. Harder. Faster. Oh, fuck, yeah..."

Lexi gasped, "I'm, oh... Fuck..."

As her orgasm began to roll through her body in a shockwave of rapture, Blaze reached for her breasts and squeezed each nipple - a little pain to mix with her pleasure. Then her pussy clenched, squeezing down hard on his cock, and he felt his orgasm begin to surge. His eyes rolled back in his head and the adrenaline that coursed through his body began to wane.

Their bodies stilled as they became swamped in ecstasy, and the madness of their crashing waves of pleasure became a sea of white noise. The only sound to break the silence was two hearts beating in time together as one.

Safe in Blaze's arms, head resting on his chest, happy and content to be held by the man she loved, Lexi floated. Half awake, half dreaming, she smiled sleepily as she traced the colorful mural he'd tattooed on his chest. It was one of her favorite things to do and each time she did she discovered something new. The scars only told a part of his story. The rest of his story was held inside – his head, his heart, his soul. It hadn't taken him long to share himself with her, and when he had, she knew it was because he had recognized similar scars within her.

Finding someone you could share yourself that way with was half the battle of finding love she supposed. If you couldn't open yourself, fully open, and share every part of your being, then how would you know whether or not you've found your soulmate?

She'd learned her lesson with Jackson. There were parts of herself she'd never really told him about, and looking back she knew, there were parts of him he'd held back as well. She guessed that was one of the pitfalls of looking at a relationship through the smitten puppy dog eyes of first love.

"You want to tell me how you're half asleep but your brain is speeding along on a rollercoaster? I thought I fucked your brains out?"

Lexi giggled and snuggled even closer to his muscular body. "Sometimes I just can't turn it off."

"Well, you need to. You need some rest."

"I know. But I need to get up and let Lucky out one more time before we call it a night."

"I've got him. You just snuggle under these covers and I'll be back before you know it."

"Okay."

Blaze slid out of bed and crept out the door as Lexi settled herself on her pillow and pulled the covers over herself. She was asleep before he made it all the way downstairs.

Staring up at the glow of the brightly shining moon, Blaze leaned on the deck rail that ran the length of the back porch and waited for the dog to take care of his business. The events of the past forty-eight hours played on a loop through his mind that pulled and tugged at his growing mental anguish. Fear and worry for Lexi, the uncertainty of what had happened and who had been involved, the absolute horror he'd felt when he'd seen her running for her life as she'd escaped the cabin only to be recaptured by her assailant. It all ate away at him until he thought he would be sick.

As he'd told the others earlier in the evening, logically he knew it wasn't his fault – or, at least not directly. But that did nothing to assuage his perceived guilt, anxiety, and depression. Then to add bonus points to the mental disorder scoreboard, there was the 'what if' that lurked around the edges. What if he hadn't gotten to her in time? What if he hadn't found her at all? What if Bradley had decided to seriously hurt her from the very first moment he'd abducted her? What if, heaven forbid, he'd actually lost the only woman he'd ever given his heart to?

Well, he supposed that he would have died right alongside her.

Scenes from his nightmare began to flash through his mind, and when he reached the point where he dove into the sea, reaching deeper and deeper as he swam into the inky darkness only to continue to come back empty-handed, the depths of his despair began to cloud his mind. And though he tried to fight against the depression that pressed in on him, he knew that it wouldn't take much to tip the scales and send him over the edge.

Taking a few deep breaths to try to clear his mind and calm his racing heart, he called for Lucky and made his way back inside and up to bed.

And though he was quite simply exhausted, it was a very long time before his mind calmed and he finally drifted off to sleep.

Chapter Fifteen

E arly the next morning Blaze's phone rang. Eyes bleary with sleep he glanced at the readout which showed the main phone line for the station. His voice was raspy when he answered.

"It's too early for phone calls, Sheriff."

"You can say that again. I came in a couple of hours ahead of shift anticipating the exact mess we have on our hands. The phones were busy off and on all night with reports of roads washed out, people stranded, and cars stuck. The towing companies are swamped. Emergency services are doing what they can to reach anyone sick, injured, or with special needs. I hate to ask you to come in with all you and Lexi have been through the past couple of days, but we sure could use your help today, especially since we're spread thin due to the search for Bradley Hayden's body."

"As much as I don't like the thought of leaving her just yet, I understand. I'll get my ass down there as soon as I can."

"Thanks. I appreciate it."

Blaze ended the call and lay there for a moment with his eyes closed as he tried to mentally prepare for the day and all the challenges that lay ahead. When he felt something heavy land on his chest and knock the breath from his lungs, he could do nothing but smile. An object dropped to the bed beside him and a moment later he felt Lucky's soft tongue begin to lick his face and greet him good morning.

"Looks like someone is happy to see you this morning." Lexi propped herself on her arm and grinned as she watched the love fest as it played out before her. The black satin sheet covering her naked body draped enticingly across her rounded breasts. Though his hands were busy rubbing on the dog, Blaze couldn't take his eyes off her.

"You're so fucking beautiful." Lexi's face lit up with a smile as she reached out to cup his chin in her hand and rubbed her fingers through his thick beard.

"I'll never get tired of hearing you say that, and I'll never get tired of seeing that look in your eyes when you do."

"I have to go to the station."

"I heard."

"That means I have to leave you."

"I know."

"Will you..."

Lexi cut him off. "I'll be fine. I promise."

"I need one more taste of you before I go."

"Then you better come take a bite," she said breathily.

The deep growl that reverberated in his chest made her chuckle and when he gave the command for the dog to get down, she threw the sheet aside and gave him a come hither look. Freed from the weight of the dog, Blaze began to roll toward her. When he rolled on top of something hard he grimaced and reached underneath him to dislodge the object. Laughing when he unearthed a dog toy, he stared at it with a raised eyebrow and crooked grin. "I think we're going to have to have a discussion with our dog about which toys we find acceptable in our bed." Lexi giggled as he tossed the toy behind him to the floor and Lucky scrambled after it.

But when Blaze reached for her once more, the giggles and laughter quickly faded into moans and gasps of pleasure.

Though the day before had wreaked havoc through-out the mountains, the bright sun shining down as Lexi watched Blaze's truck round a bend in the driveway gave the landscape around her a beautiful glow. Towering trees had lost limbs and leaves that had only just begun to appear, but the leafy greens that remained attached, still daintily dripped glistening droplets. She took a deep breath and tasted the first true hints of spring in the air. It won't be long, she thought, until the trees recover, the grass turns dark green, and the flowers begin to bloom.

Seasons come and seasons go, she thought, and she loved them all. Each was necessary in her mind. You need the cold and snow of winter to make the spring bloom with promise. You need the mild temperatures and colorful displays of spring to prepare you for the heat of summer. You need the high temperatures and searing sun of summer to make you appreciate the cooler temperatures of the fall. And you needed the last hints of warmth from fall to prepare you for the harshness of winter.

The seasons in the area of Kentucky she'd grown up in were mild in their changes. She had discovered since moving to the mountains she enjoyed those season changes much more than she ever had in Kentucky. The greens were greener. The colors more vibrant, and when autumn arrived, the burnt umber, red, and gold of the changing leaves was considerably more drastic. Living on her mountain was a colorful wonderland that pleased her artistic soul. And while part of her missed her hometown and surrounding areas, she was far happier here than she had ever been living in the Bluegrass state.

She hadn't set foot in Kentucky since the day she'd closed out her parent's estates, and though she had no reason to go back now, part of her wondered if anything had significantly changed in the years she'd been gone. Were they still having their tiny town festivals? Were the football stadiums still packed every week as the students cheered on their teams for Friday Night Lights? Were those same teenagers sneaking out on summer nights to get drunk in cornfields? Were they snuggling into the corners of hayride trucks and stealing kisses in the fall? And while she had no desire to go back, it did bring her wonderfully happy memories to think back to her own rights of passage.

Reminiscing always seemed to settle her soul and after the past few turbulent days, the walk down memory lane helped to center her. Taking another cleansing breath, she opened her eyes and looked around for the dog. Seeing him wandering the treeline, she called to him and he came running.

Being by herself had never bothered her, but she now found herself looking left and right, her eyes darting around the yard, constantly on the lookout for something amiss. Anxious nerves hummed beneath her skin. As much as she wanted to believe she was unconcerned about being alone, and as much as she'd done to convince Blaze she was alright by herself, she couldn't help the occasional niggling thoughts to be cautious. Seeing nothing concerning as she looked around one more time, she exhaled a deep breath she hadn't been aware she'd been holding.

"Alright, Lucky. We have work to do." He looked up at her with adoring eyes and waited patiently for her to continue. "You see all these s-t-i-c-k-s? We're going to play a game. I'm going to say the word and you bring some to me, okay?" She laughed as the dog barked his approval just as if he understood exactly what she meant. "We'll make us a couple of piles and then we'll gather them all up and get them out of the way. We've got to clean up this yard, okay?"

Another bark of agreement and she gave the command, "Lucky! Stick. Fetch!"

They worked in tandem until the yard was cleared and once again spotless.

"That's better." Lexi absently petted the dog as she took a final glance around the property. "How about we go inside and get a treat? Then maybe," she yawned, "you and I will take a little nap. I think maybe every-thing is finally catching up with me. Come on, Lucky! Let's go!"

With a bark of approval, he took off running toward the door and Lexi wasted no time locking them inside before settling in for a restful afternoon.

"Thank God the phone has finally stopped ringing. Hopefully, this last call will take care of everyone." Blaze stood looking out the door of the police station as he downed the last of an energy drink. It had been a long, hard day of washed-out roads, rescues, and damage assessments. For the most part, it was neighbor help-ing neighbor and things had gone smoothly for all that they'd faced. For the most part. There had been a couple of incidents of high tempers and Blaze grimaced when he thought of dealing with the latest call for a couple of hotheads.

"Why don't you go on home? I know how anxious you are to get back to Lexi. I can take this one and then I can go home myself."

"I appreciate that Sheriff, but I don't want to leave you in a bind."

"Blaze. It's all good. Go take care of your girl. Besides, it's just Old Man Jeffries and Mr. Handy. Again. There's no telling what all has got those two riled up now, but you know how they are. By the time I get there, they'll probably be best friends again. Go. Give her a hug from me and take the day off tomorrow. Hell. After what we just went through, we could all use a day off. Besides, once we're sure things are back to some semblance of normal around here, I'm going to need you to be on top of your game. We've still got a drug ring to break up."

Relief floated through his system. He hadn't wanted to leave Lexi. The very idea of her being out of his sight so soon after her abduction had kept him on edge all day. "You sure? I can put in a little time on that now and see if I can round up some more leads. "

"Go. We'll deal with that soon enough."

"Alright. I won't argue. I've tried to give her a bit of space today so she wouldn't think I was hovering or overreacting. The way we busted our asses being busy today helped, but I'm ready to get back to her. You know, I never thought I would let someone in the way I have Lexi, but I simply can't imagine my life without her." A grin of happiness brightened his tired features.

"Love is a wonderful thing. A frightening, over-whelming thing at times, but still a wonderful blessing. Now get out of here."

"I'm gone!"

Blaze quickly gathered his things and hurried out the door to begin the lengthy drive home.

Lexi stretched her body as she floated along on the dregs of her dream. The nap had been just what she needed though she now found herself having trouble waking. Every time she thought she was surfacing, she was taken back under.

Her memories of her past and the time she'd spent reminiscing that morning continued to float through her mind as she slept. Dreams of actual events overlaid with new people and different outcomes tricked her mind and left her confused but curious. A quick succession of memories of one of those hayrides she loved, one where she'd been huddled together with Jackson, now ran through her mind with images of Blaze and his warm brown eyes staring down at her with adoration.

Then, a pre-game bonfire with everyone cheering on the football team. Lexi saw herself in the band, playing her trumpet and cheering right along with the rest of the crowd. She saw herself as she looked over to the flatbed truck where the football team stood looking out on their supporters, hyping the crowd. Jackson should be up there, she thought, but confusion swept through her when she couldn't find him. Then from out of the corner of her eye she saw Blaze as he swaggered toward her with a gleam of longing in his eyes.

Happiness soared through her - heart, mind, body, and soul.

Odd, she thought, I can almost smell the smoke from the bonfire. The woodsy scent tickled her senses as the dream became redolent with scent memory. The longer she dreamed, the stronger the smell became.

She coughed, her body reacting to the swirling haze of smoke rising from the roaring fire in the center of the crowd. When her lungs began to ache, a feeling of dread joined her confusion.

Once again she tried to surface from the dream, to escape from the strange combination of memories of the past merging with the present but found herself slipping back under. When a loud bark sounded next to her, she managed to open her eyes and peer through a tiny slit at Lucky next to her on the bed. The dog began to bark louder, pouncing on the bed with excitement in an attempt to get her attention. Confusion swept through her as she propped herself on an elbow and began to try to blink away the haze clouding her vision.

It only took a brief moment for her to realize they were in trouble.

Smoke filled the bedroom and began to clog her lungs. It hadn't been a dream – rather a strange combination of dream and reality. As she coughed harder, her eyes began to burn. Awake, but groggy, she stumbled from the bed on wobbly legs and tried to orient herself. Her head began to whirl with dizziness and she grabbed onto the edge of the dresser to steady herself.

Lucky bounded off the bed after her and began to nip at the arm of the long-sleeved shirt she wore as he continued to try to get her attention. When his teeth latched on to the material he began to tug, urging her to go. Get out. Run to safety.

Lexi shook her head, confusion and panic continuing to disorient her as she staggered to the doorway. The sleep fog in her brain slowly began to clear even as more smoke began to roll in under the edge of the closed door. She started to open the door but caught herself and placed her hand against the wood to feel for heat. Finding none, she slowly turned the handle and eased the heavy wood open a slit to peer out.

Though the smoke was heavier and thicker in the hallway and the temperature obviously higher, no flames were visible from the bedroom. With one hand on the dog's collar, she hurried to the stairs and peered down into the living room. Orange and red flames licked at the edge of the living room carpet, the fire spreading from the direction of the kitchen, cutting off access to the front door as well as the door to the back yard. The combination of heat and fear had sweat trickling down her back and her heart raced as she tried to figure out what to do.

The only course of action was to hope the fire hadn't spread to her studio. With any luck, she'd be able to break through the heavy double-paned windows to escape. If the fire had spread to her studio, though, the only other option would be to go back to the bedroom and jump. The slope of the A-frame would help with the height, but it would still be a long way down to the ground and there was Lucky to consider. She refused to leave him behind.

Taking a deep breath and steeling herself for what she might find, she hurried down the stairs, Lucky at her side, and rushed to the studio. Once again she felt the wooden panel of the door before she opened it. The air of the studio was thick with smoke and she could hardly see through the haze, but no flames awaited them. She rushed inside and closed the door.

Looking left and right, she searched for something heavy enough she could use to beat against the glass panels. Various instruments sat around the room as well as her recording equipment, but it was the metal microphone stand that caught her attention.

Reaching for the pole, she dislodged the microphone and hurried toward the window. Rearing back, she began to swing it like a bat, connecting with the panel as hard as she could. Corners she thought, hit the corners as they are supposed to be weak spots. Each hit reverberated up her arms and made them ache with her efforts. And while she tried desperately to escape, the fire roared on, growing and increasing in size and strength.

And though her lungs burned as the smoke continued to fill the room and her arms began to tire from the force of her blows, she didn't stop. She wouldn't stop. She had too much to live for, had been through too much, and wasn't about to give up when the future she wanted with the man she loved was only a hair's breadth away.

It had taken courage and determination to survive, to learn how to live after losing Jackson and her parents. It had taken trust and openness to learn how to love again after closing her heart and soul to the world around her. Nothing and nobody was going to take the life she wanted, the future she deserved from her now. She simply wouldn't allow it.

The light of day had begun to fade as Blaze rounded the last few turns and climbed the final steep incline up the mountain toward home. With the window down and his music blaring, he exhaled a sigh of relief at being so close to home. He needed Lexi in his arms, a beer in hand, and his feet propped on the coffee table while they shared a few quiet moments together.

As he drove the first hint of smoke wafted in through the window and he wrinkled his nose in confusion. It was a little late in the year for anyone to be using their fireplace. It was then that he noticed a haze in the air and his heart began to trip in his chest. Alarm bells began to ring and he gave the truck some gas as the urgency to get home began to throb a steady beat within his body.

The further he went the thicker the smoke became. He reached the turn for the driveway and floored it, rushing up the serpentine drive, taking the switchbacks and twisty lane up to the house as fast as he could. When the house came into view his stomach pitched and panic that had only been tickling the edges of his heart roared through his body.

The house, the beautiful home that Lexi had built as her safe haven now stood almost completely engulfed in flames. His chocolate eyes widened with fear; he couldn't believe what he was seeing.

The woman he loved, whom he simply could not live without, was nowhere in sight while the home they shared slowly began to crumble beneath the scorching heat and searing flames of the inferno.

Blaze barely had the truck stopped before he jumped out and raced toward the burning building.

Chapter Sixteen

When a spiderweb of cracks appeared in the glass, Lexi felt the first stirrings of relief. She'd spent an exorbitant amount of money on the floor-to-ceiling windows to make sure they were soundproof, strong, and could withstand the test of time. It's nice, she thought, to know that sometimes you do actually get what you pay for.

She felt as if she'd been beating on the picture window for hours instead of minutes. Each blow now sent pain in shockwaves up her arms, but seeing the beginnings of a breakthrough urged her to continue, to hit harder, faster. With each hit the cracks spread further and further. Beside her, Lucky danced and barked in excitement.

She reared back once more and swung with all her might. Finally, a decent-sized hole appeared in the glass. As she went to swing again, movement caught her attention and she almost fell to her knees in relief.

There, on the other side of the glass, stood Blaze.

The tears she'd been holding back began to stream down her face.

With the front and back doors fully engulfed in flames, Blaze ran around to the side of the house hoping he could find a point of entry that would allow him to get to Lexi. Seeing her trying to break out the window relieved him but he could tell by her body language when she spotted him, she was almost at the end of her rope. Her strength had begun to wane. The mental and physical exhaustion she was experiencing was close to causing her to fall apart.

He saw where she'd made progress on breaking out the window and determined to get to her and get her out, began working from the outside. He stripped out of his T-shirt and wrapped it around his hand to offer some protection from the glass.

Quickly, he began punching his fist into the cracks. Three hard punches and the structural integrity of the glass finally failed. Shards of glass began to splinter and fall. His muscles rippled as he continued to hit and knock out the glass until he began to make headway into enlarging the hole. It didn't take long until the opening was large enough that Lucky, anxious to get out and get to Blaze took a leap and landed on the grass next to him. Then, with a few more punches, Lexi quickly followed, launching herself into Blaze's arms. He caught her in a bear hug and began to run toward the edge of the property.

"I've got you. I've got you, Angel. Let me see. Let me see you. Are you hurt? Oh God! I've got you and I'm not ever letting go."

They dropped to the ground and she curled tighter around him even as he tried to ease her back to look her over for injuries. "Come on, Angel. Lean back here and let me look at you. Are you hurt?"

Sobs continued to wrack her body but she raised her face enough that he could see the vivid green of her eyes, frightened and darting around as she shook her head in answer to his question. "I'm okay. I'm okay. Can you just... hold me? Just hold me, Blaze."

He hugged her closely. "I'll never let go."

"The house..."

"I know, Angel. I know. I need to call it in and I need to try to contain it as much as I can until help can get here."

"We're going to lose everything." The sadness in her voice gutted him.

"No. No, we aren't. We've got each other." He glanced over to where Lucky lay on the grass, his head on his paws and staring at the two of them as he patiently awaited his turn for attention. "We've got Lucky. Everything else can be replaced. All that matters is that you're safe."

He watched as she swiped absently at her tear and soot-streaked face. "Call it in. I'll hook a hose up to the well and start trying to contain it."

"Nope. I'll call it in, but you are doing nothing right now but sitting here and breathing."

"But..."

"No," he cut her off. The stern look he gave her made her nod her head in agreement as he reached for his phone.

The soaking rains from the day before worked in their favor, and though the house was a complete loss, they were able to keep the fire from spreading further. Now, as the volunteer firemen continued to shoot streams onto the smoldering remains of the house, Blaze stoically looked on, dividing his attention between the house and the back of the ambulance where Lexi sat being evaluated. She wore an oxygen mask as a precaution while the EMT on duty tended to her minor cuts and scrapes.

Darkness had fully fallen and it was only by the flood-lights of the emergency crews illuminating the area that he was able to see anything.

"It has been a hell of a few days."

Blaze turned toward the man next to him with a raised eyebrow. "You can say that again, Sheriff."

"Fire investigator will be out in the morning when he's got some light to see by. But going by the look on your face I'm going to say you don't believe this was an accident or natural causes."

"Not at all."

"Shit." The sheriff shook his head in disbelief as he watched the firefighters call all clear and begin to roll up their hoses. It didn't take long for them to begin to break down their mobile command center. Fast and efficient – just what he liked to see in emergency personnel. "You think it has something to do with the drug ring, don't you?"

"That would be my first guess."

"Mine too. If that's the case, these sons of bitches just keep adding to their charges. When we take them down, they're not getting back up."

"Agreed."

"I sense a but there, son."

"But, what if my first instinct is wrong? What if this wasn't the drug ring? I've been wrong before."

"You've been right a whole hell of a lot more than you've been wrong."

"Maybe." Blaze cut his eyes toward Lexi as she began to walk in their direction. "Let's table this for now. She's had enough."

The Sheriff nodded his head in understanding. Blaze held out his arm to her and Lexi tucked herself beneath his shoulder as she wrapped her arms around his waist and held on tightly.

"I think it's time we got away from here." Lexi nodded her head in agreement.

"I guess we'll have to go find us a room somewhere until we can get things sorted out."

"Actually, you have a place to stay, and not just for the night."

"Oh, now Sheriff, I appreciate it, but we couldn't put you out that way." Lexi smiled kindly at him.

"While we would love to have the two of you stay with us, we don't have the room. No. This offer, actually, this insistence comes from Ms. Eliza." Reaching in his pocket he pulled out a set of keys and handed them to Blaze. "She has a fully furnished rental in town. The couple who were renting it moved out about a month ago and she hasn't been able to replace them yet. She said to tell you the place is yours as long as you need it."

"That's very generous of her, but..."

"Nope. If you want to argue about it, son, you can take it up with her. I, for one, am not going to be the one to push her buttons. And the two of you even thinking about turning her down will definitely push her buttons. Your call, but you can leave me right out of the middle of it. I'm only the messenger and delivery service."

Blaze bounced the keys in his hand and caught them before putting them in his pocket. "Alright. For now, anyway, we'll accept."

"Good. She said there's everything you need other than personal items and she was going to see about stocking some food in the fridge and pantry. You should have everything right down to fresh linens, which I'm told she and her sister went over and washed in anticipation of your arrival. You'll have a freshly made bed to rest in tonight, kids."

With a nod at the Sheriff, Blaze looked down at Lexi and kissed her forehead. "Ready?" His heart broke a bit more as Lexi looked over to where her home had once stood. Battling back tears, she nodded, and with one last look at the charred remnants, whistled for the dog.

As they started down the driveway Blaze tried not to look in the rearview mirror but found himself doing so all the same. He knew he was going to have to do some digging to get to the source of the fire. He just hoped that the cause wasn't yet another ghost from his past rearing its ugly head. And with that thought, a shiver of warning and trepidation slithered its way down his spine.

He'd taken a chance. Not only with setting the fire but with hanging around to watch the house burn with Lexi closed up inside. It had been a risk, but so worth it. Watching Blaze come speeding up the drive and losing his mind when he saw both entrances blocked by a wall of flames had brought a smile to his face. Seeing him run from one door to the other and back again, horror on his face had brought him a sick sense of pleasure. He'd only been slightly disappointed when between the two of them they'd managed to get her out of the house and to safety. That's alright, he thought. It doesn't matter how long it takes or how much damage is inflicted along the way. There was hell to pay and he would get his due – one way or another.

One thing he hadn't expected, was the other set of eyes he'd found watching the house in fascination as it had begun to burn, the flames quickly engulfing the structure. Definitely an unexpected development, but one he planned to use as fully as possible. Yes, he thought, he would use whatever means necessary, and if that meant recruiting an extremely unexpected player to his team, then so be it. The enemy of an enemy could easily be swayed to be an ally.

All you needed to do was dangle the right bait in front of their face.

"That's twice I thought I'd lost you within a twenty-four-hour time period." Blaze's large body curled around Lexi as they stretched out for the night, her head resting comfortably on his arm. Exhaustion weighed heavily on both of them and worry wound its way through their voices as they discussed the fire.

"You've been very tight-lipped with your thoughts on how and why the fire started. You've never hidden anything from me. Please don't start now." Unshed tears tickled the corners of her eyes as she tried to make sense of all that had happened to them.

"I'm not hiding anything. I promise. It's more that I'm grasping at straws. I'm pretty certain that someone set the fire, Angel. There were what appeared to be two starting points. I can't see anything happening naturally that way. The fire inspector will be out in the morning and we'll get a better idea once he's had a look around. But going off it being intentional, my best guess is that it's related to this drug ring we're trying to break up."

"One of those dangers of being involved with a law enforcement officer."

"Yeah. I'm sorry Lexi."

"What on earth are you sorry for?"

"If this is why, if me trying to do my job has once again put you in danger, I don't know if I can forgive myself."

"Michael." Lexi rolled so she lay facing him and took his bearded face in her hands. "There is nothing to forgive. We both knew the dangers going into this. No matter what the outcome, we'll handle it. We'll handle it and we'll handle it the best way I know how. Together."

"You have to be frightened out of your mind, Angel."

Lexi nodded her head. "Yeah, I'm scared. But as long as I have you, I can make it through anything."

"It just seems like we can't get our footing. Here you were living this peaceful life up on that mountain, doing your thing and not worrying over every little thing that came along. Then I crashed into the mountain and brought six different kinds of hell with me."

"Stop." Lexi propped herself on her elbow so she could look down into his eyes and make her point. "You crashed into my mountain and you opened my heart. You crashed into my world and helped me to live again. You crashed into my existence and helped me realize all I was doing was going through the motions. I was content until you came along. Now I'm happy. I was a void of emotion until you came along. Now I can feel again. I was closed off to everyone and everything around me. Now I have all I've ever wanted. You. Michael Blaizure, are all I want, all I need. You are all I have ever hoped for in this life."

"Your home..." Placing a finger against his lips she silenced him.

"I loved that house. I was able to pour myself into it when my world crumbled around me. It took my mind off the fact that I was all alone. It was my haven. It sheltered me when I needed it. It gave me a place to hide from the world. It was what I needed when I needed it." She sighed as she shook her head. "Don't you see? That was a house. A structure. Something that could be replaced. You. You are my home. No matter where life takes us, no matter what it throws our way, as long as I have you, I have my home."

He pulled her down to him and claiming her lips, poured himself and his love for her into the kiss. Sweet but powerful, he offered himself – heart, mind, body, and soul. Then he rolled her beneath him and with his eyes locked on hers, slid his cock slowly into her heat. Home, he thought, was many things to many people. For them? Home was and would always be their two hearts joined together for eternity.

The day dawned bright and clear, and though the sun shone down on the charred remains of the house, smoke still lingered in the air and left a thin, hazy film to peer through. A handful of people stood in a circle, somberly watching and waiting for the fire inspector to complete his evaluation. When at last he walked toward them with clipboard in hand, it was with a resigned look on his face.

"Well, folks, I hate to tell you this, but your suspicions are correct." Blaze wrapped his arm around Lexi's waist and pulled her tightly against him as they waited for the inspector to continue. "This was definitely not from natural causes. The fire was set at two different points – the front door, the back door. I see traces of an accelerant. The lab will confirm but I suspect it was something as simple as gasoline. As far as I can tell, they doused both entrances and then tossed a match. Whoever did this wanted to make it very difficult for anyone inside to have an easy escape. Again, I've got some samples to send off to the lab and it will take a few days to get that back even with me pushing for priority. But, I'll let you know as soon as I know." Looking back and forth between Blaze and Lexi he issued his warning. "If I were the two of you, I'd be very cautious. I can't say for sure they were trying to take one or both of you out of the game, but they sure were trying to slow ya down."

"Duly noted. Thanks for coming out so quickly."

As the inspector walked away, those who remained began talking and speculating.

"With no other obvious leads, I say we do some follow-up on the drug ring. We've still got that asshole dealer locked up because nobody could come up with bail money for him. We'll have to wait for his attorney to show up, but I think it's time to question him again." Sheriff Kaminski looked back and forth between his two deputies.

"He's mine." The steely edge that rang in Blaze's voice spoke volumes.

"Oh, hell no, Deputy. You're way too close to this now." Irritation radiated from Blaze as he tried to control his anger. He'd never done well sitting on the sidelines while others made the calls and did the work. "Deputy Shaver, he's ours. Let's head down and tag team him."

With a grin, Deputy Shaver's enthusiasm for interrogation radiated across his face. "You got it, Sheriff."

"What do you want me to do? I have to do something. Anything." Blaze looked around as impotent frustration hardened his features.

"Not today. Today, you two do what you need to set up that house you're in and take care of the logistics with this one." The Sheriff gestured behind him. "Insurance is going to be a bitch to deal with so you may as well get started while you're waiting for the official report. Rest. You both look a sight better than you did last night, but you still need some rest."

"Don't worry, Sheriff," Lexi smiled. "I'll make sure you don't see him again until tomorrow morning."

"Good. Let's roll."

As trucks disappeared down the drive, Lexi stepped in front of Blaze and wrapped her arms around him. "I know you want in on this. The energy is vibrating off of you in shock waves. Not today, okay? We need the break."

"I just feel like I need to be doing something to help."

"You are. Having you with me today is a huge help. I need that. I need you with me."

Blaze sighed. "Well, if that isn't a sucker punch. You just played dirty and you know what? I think I liked it."

"Good," Lexi laughed, "because you know," Lexi trailed her fingers up his chest and hooked her arms around his neck as she smiled up at him flirtatiously, "I like to play dirty sometimes."

The guttural growl that rumbled from deep within him made her grin. "Well, maybe I'll work on using some of this pent-up energy in other ways."

One moment she was standing and in the next Blaze had scooped her up and over his shoulder. She squeaked out her surprise and delight. "What on earth are you doing?"

"Well, you said you liked to play dirty. So do I." Walking quickly to his truck he opened the tailgate and sat Lexi down. "Sit and don't you dare move until I tell you to."

"Oh. Really? Right now?" Lexi glanced around. It wasn't as if they'd never made love outside before. In fact, they did it often. But for some reason, the absence of the house made her feel extremely exposed. "Ummm, okay."

Blaze disappeared to the front of his truck and came back a moment later with bungee cords.

"What are you...?"

"I'm hungry, Angel. And you and your sweet pussy are the only things that can sate my appetite." Wrapping her wrist with a bungee, Blaze took the ends with hooks and attached them to the bed of the truck. When he repeated the process for her other wrist, Lexi's heart began to pound. "There. Plenty of give - you could get loose if you wanted. But believe me, Angel, you're not going to want to. Lay back and hold on tight."

Warm liquid flooded her jeans and she moaned in anticipation. A moment later she felt her shoes being removed with her jeans quickly following. "Now, spread those legs for me." As she let her legs fall to the sides, she heard the deep growl of his again, and her body began to tremble uncontrollably. "Mmmm... look how wet you are."

"Oh, God, Blaze...you're killing me."

"The other way around, Angel. Other way around."

Then he dove for her, burying his face in her sweetness, coating his beard with her arousal. With long, slow licks, he excited as he savored, drinking her in, and going back for more. He teased her clit, circling, flicking, and lapping at her, relishing her as a treat for his senses. When he sucked her in, he pushed her over the edge. And though she flew with the orgasm, he continued to take her higher. He never let up, never stopped, and pulled three orgasms from her before his own need took control and he let his jeans fall to his knees and pulled her to the edge of the tailgate to bury himself deep inside.

Mania set in as he pumped deeply, working both of their bodies to madness. The sound of his voice alone was enough to push her to the top once more as his cock thrust against her G-spot repeatedly. "Oh God! There it is..." When at last they came, they did so together. And though she was flying once more, Lexi watched in fascination as Blaze's eyes crossed then rolled back in his head as pleasure consumed him and his body stilled as he filled her with cum.

When he looked into her eyes once more, a devilish grin split her face and she used her pelvic muscles to clamp down on his cock, squeezing him with all her might.

"Oh God! Oh Fuck!"

Lexi laughed, full and robust, "I told you I like to play dirty. I win."

"Oh, Love, we both win. Believe me. We both win!"

Chapter Seventeen

Later that evening as the dusk of twilight began to settle in the deep valleys between mountain ridges, two cars drove down a semi-dark gravel road. Head to head they met and as the beams from their headlights blared against each other and illuminated the area, the drivers stood between their vehicles and had a meeting of minds.

"I thought you were gone."

"I thought you were an upstanding member of this community."

"Looks like we were both wrong."

"By now you know all about me. I'm curious though, why are you doing it?"

"He's ruining my plans and any future I have hoped and planned for."

"Interesting way to go about it."

"It's working."

"My way is better."

"And that's why you're standing here. I think maybe you need to rethink your methods."

"Listen, fucker, it's going to happen. One way or another I'm making it happen. The question is, do you want in? Or does it go too far against your dark gray code of ethics and morality?"

"I'm listening."

"That's what I thought."

Thoughts and ideas were tossed back and forth and before long a plan was in place. They parted ways, each going in the opposite direction from whence they came, with the knowledge that the last day Michael "Blaze" Blaisure would be gracing the earth was fast approaching.

Two days later Blaze stormed into the station, a determined storm ready to wreak havoc on anyone and anything in its path. He went directly to Sheriff Kaminski's desk and as he approached, the sheriff looked up and grimaced.

"Blaze."

"Sheriff. Fill me in."

"Well, it's nice to see you, too."

"Come on. Cut the bull. I took my days off. I'm ready. I need to do something."

"I get that, son. I do. At this point, there isn't much more we can do. The report from the lab isn't in yet. Once we know for sure what the accelerant was we can do some more digging."

"Alright. What about the search for Bradley's body?"

"Unfortunately we've come up empty-handed. There are no signs of his body anywhere. It could be his body is buried under tons of mud, dirt, and debris. I have a team out looking but it can't be our main priority right now."

Guilt crossed Blaze's face as he considered all the sheriff had told him. "Have you spoken to his parents yet?"

"No. No, I haven't. I'm not comfortable doing that just yet. I'm hoping we can find his body first. It's hard enough on parents losing a child, but not having a body to say goodbye to is worse."

"Yeah, I guess I can see that."

"And the drug ring?"

"Ah! There we have a development. Deputy Shaver and I interviewed the pusher again but didn't get anywhere. His Public Defender pretty well squashed every attempt we made to get information out of him. But, Shaver managed to take down another perp. He was at the park. He just happened upon a deal and managed to bring him in."

"Dealing to another kid?"

"Yeah. We've got to get this wrapped up, and soon. I refuse to see this area turn from a quaint little town to a drug haven."

"Did you get anything from him?"

"No. Same deal. He's keeping quiet. We're going to have the Feds breathing down our necks soon."

"Damn it."

"We'll get him back out this afternoon and see if we can get anywhere. He hasn't lawyered up yet, so there's a chance. I assume you want in?"

"Oh, absolutely! I've got to do something. I'm antsy and if I don't do something about one or more of these cases I'm going to crawl right out of my skin."

"How's Lexi?"

"Considering all she's been through? She's doing alright. She's strong. She's stronger than she believes herself to be. Some people would crumble under the pressure of all the hell she's been through, but not her. She's fucking amazing."

"I can see that. So, tell me this, Deputy, just when the hell are the two of you going to set a damn date? Y'all have been engaged for a long time now. Don't you think it's time to make it official?"

Blaze grinned cheekily. "Yeah. We're long overdue for setting a date. Maybe I'll address that tonight. It would be a happy direction for her thoughts – mine too, for that matter."

"My wife is going to be pleased to hear it. She's been itching to dig into something like that and she's been dropping hints about stopping by and talking to Lexi about it."

"Oh boy!"

Sheriff Kaminski shook his head. "Son, you don't know the half of it. We've got calls of chaos all over the place. A fight over at the school, a semi that jackknifed trying to cut a turn too closely, and even a report of a stolen car. I haven't looked but we must be getting close to a full moon."

At that moment the phone on his desk rang. "Yeah." He listened for a moment and almost immediately rolled his eyes. "Alright. I'll send someone over." He hung up the phone, leaned back in his comfy chair, and ran a hand down his face in frustration. "They're at it again."

"Oh, hell. What now?"

"Old man Jeffries is refusing to honor his bet on the WVU vs Penn State game from March Madness last month. Mr. Handy is riled, to say the least – says he's been patient long enough and it's time to pay up. They're over at the diner again, damn it."

"Relax. I've got it. It'll give me something to do until we pull the dealer out this afternoon."

"Fine. Go." He shooed him toward the front door of the station. Blaze had just pushed the door open when he heard the sheriff call out, "Hey! Bring me back a piece of pie to go with my lunch while you're there!"

"I got you, Sheriff!" Blaze grinned and slipped on his sunglasses as he walked out into the bright sunshine.

Lexi put a load of laundry in the dryer and turned to start the next load. She'd just started the washer when she heard a knock on the front door. Lucky let out a series of loud barks as if the knock on the door wasn't enough to let Lexi know they had company. She looked at the time and then at the front door in confusion.

"Alright, alright. I get it Lucky!" Lexi reached for the door handle and as her hand latched onto the cool, smooth metal, she paused. A flutter of panic made her rethink opening the door without knowing who was on the other side. Cautiously and quietly she raised on tiptoe and peeked through the peephole. When she saw the woman waiting on the other side she smiled, relieved to see her friend. Quickly she opened the door to let her inside.

"Sandra! What a pleasant surprise! Come on in." Lexi held the door for the sheriff's wife who carried in a laundry basket full of household items.

"I hope you don't mind. I had a conversation with Ms. Eliza yesterday and she told me you could probably use a few things around the rental. I was out doing some shopping this morning and found some stuff to help make this place a bit homier for the two of you."

"That's so nice, but you really didn't have to do that."

"Nonsense! What are friends for?"

"Well, we appreciate it. I was just about to pour myself some tea can I get you something?"

"Actually, I have a few things I'd love to talk with you about so, yes, a glass of tea would be lovely if you have the time."

"Sure! Come on back." The women walked to the back of the house and before long they were huddled around the kitchen table talking out ideas for Blaze and Lexi's wedding.

Two hours later, Lexi closed the door behind her friend and leaned against it with a sigh of relief. She was grateful, truly grateful for Sandra and their friendship but convincing her friend that she wanted to keep the wedding a small, intimate affair without too much fanfare had been an exhausting task. Somehow she'd managed to talk her down from a huge affair at the local Baptist church to a simple outdoor ceremony. Now she was exhausted. Reining in someone so excited about vintage wedding invitations with foil lettering and deckled edging had been a task in and of itself. That had only been the beginning.

From invitations to cakes and flowers and shopping for wedding dresses, it had taken all the aural skills Lexi possessed to redirect her friend to the simple wedding she truly wanted. Before the house burned, Lexi had wanted to have the wedding in her backyard. Now, all that remained of her beautiful home was charred timber and ashes. Sandra had been pleased that Lexi had jumped on the idea of having the wedding at the local park where the trails bloomed with one flower or another throughout the spring, summer, and fall months. With tentative plans in place to share with Blaze, there was only one thing left to be decided on and it required her fiance's input just as much as hers.

A date.

Lexi pulled up a calendar on her newly acquired phone and began looking at their schedules. When she heard a knock on her door once more, she smiled. Lucky began to raise a ruckus again. She hurried to the door to give Sandra a hard time for not having made it around the block before coming back with more ideas. Lucky continued to bark and a low growl began to rumble from his chest.

"Oh, now, Lucky. Quiet! Sit!" She reached the door and without giving a thought to anything else, opened it with a smile on her face. Her beautiful smile faded instantly and horror replaced the happiness that had only moments before radiated across her features. Lucky charged the door and the man who stood on the threshold raised his arm, aimed, and fired. The helpless yelp that tore from the throat of the dog ripped Lexi's heart from her chest as she screamed in fear. Lucky's body fell to the floor with a loud thump and stilled as red began to bloom on his chest and puddle beneath him.

In the blink of an eye, the Ruger outfitted with a silencer was aimed in her direction. "Not another peep from you."

Lexi gasped and covered her mouth as tears streamed down her face. She made a move to go to Lucky but when she heard a menacing warning, she froze in place.

"Don't. Move."

"H—?" Lexi looked up into the face of the man she and everyone else assumed was dead.

"I said, shut up. How did I survive?" Bradley smiled menacingly as he entered the house and shut the door behind him. "I'm not without my bumps, bruises, cuts and scrapes. When the cliff gave way and I fell, I landed on a ledge that had a small overhang tucked back against the side of the mountain. I was able to roll and escape the worst of the mudslide. Once the storm calmed again, I was able to slowly pick my way down the side of the mountain. I finally reached a road and I walked for miles and miles. Eventually, I found a car to steal, hotwired it, and got back to business."

Horrified as to what was about to happen, Lexi stared wide-eyed as Bradley approached her. She saw it coming. As the ceiling lights softly glinted off the sheen of the gun, Lexi braced herself for impact. With a downward strike, pain shot through her head and the world went dark.

Blaze walked out of Ma's Diner and chuckled as he looked down at the load he carried. Leave it to Ma he thought as he began to drool over the pies she'd sent him back to the station with. Bless her, she'd sent two whole pies - chocolate for the sheriff and pecan for him as her thanks for getting the situation under control and helping two old men remember why they had been friends for more than sixty years.

He turned to return to the station when a shiver of unease skated down his spine. He stopped in his tracks and looked around in confusion. When the feeling continued, his heart began to thud in his chest and an inner voice told him to return to the rental to check in with Lexi. As the house was only two blocks from the diner, he changed directions and quickly made his way toward their temporary home.

Rows of quaint homes lined both sides of the street. The two-story home painted a bright and cheery yellow was normally a welcoming sight with its tall oaks offering shade and a winding walkway that led to the covered front porch and the soft blue of the front door. As he approached he noticed the slight swaying of the bench swing as the soft breeze wafted through the air. When he saw the front door slightly ajar he froze in place.

He wanted to spring into action but years and years of training cautioned him about rushing in. He sat the pies down on the porch and drew his Glock from its holster. As quietly as possible, he stepped to the door and eased it open.

The sight that reached his eyes sent fear coursing through his body. An end table lay on its side in the living room. Glass shards from a broken vase glittered across the hardwood floor and dark droplets of blood ominously painted a gruesome scene. Lucky lay in a puddle of blood, eyes closed and unmoving. Lexi was nowhere in sight. Silence echoed throughout the house and left him assured that she was either seriously injured somewhere upstairs, or she was no longer in the house. Something told him it was that latter. He wanted to run to the dog but knew he needed to check the rest of the house.

He hurried upstairs and cleared each room before rushing back down to check on the dog. He pulled his phone from his pocket and dialed the station as he kneeled next to the lifeless animal. Relief tore through him when he was able to detect faint, slow and shallow breaths coming from his friend. He made his report, concise and to the point as he tried to keep his wits about him. Instantly he heard the unmistakable sound of sirens and knew that help was on the way. He dialed the vet to prepare them, and scooped Lucky in his arms and carried him out the door.

Sheriff Kaminski came into view, tires screeching as he rounded the corner, sirens blaring and lights flashing. His truck had just come to a stop when another car came flying around the corner. Blaze was unsurprised to see Ms. Eliza come to a screeching halt directly behind the sheriff. She jumped out of the front seat and opened the back door.

"Put him in the back, Deputy! I'll take him over to the clinic! Hurry!"

Overwhelmed with the love the matronly little woman constantly showed him and Lexi, his breath shuddered in his chest. He rushed to the car and gently laid Lucky in the backseat.

"Thank you, Ms. Eliza."

"Thank me later!" She slammed the door, climbed back behind the wheel, and was gone before he knew it. He turned back to the house and quickly ushered Sheriff Kaminski inside.

"What the hell, Blaze?"

"I wish to fuck I knew, Sheriff."

"No forced entry. She let whoever this was into the house."

"I agree. It doesn't appear Lucky moved at all after he was shot so the blood splatters over there have to be Lexi's." Blaze ran a hand over his bald head and down his face in frustration, anxious with worry over the woman he simply could not live without and their four-legged family member. "Where should we—" Blaze's phone rang and he looked at the readout. Unknown number. With his heart racing, he answered.

"I have your girl. Again."

Blaze's eyes widened in shock and fear before he growled a response. "Where are you?"

With an evil laugh Bradley continued, "Oh, I'm sure you'd like to know. We're doing this my way. It's time for you and I to have a conversation. The park. Two o'clock. Come alone and take the White Oak path. We'll be waiting."

Silence thickened the air as the call cut off and Blaze looked to his friend and mentor for direction.

"Well?"

"He's alive. He's got Lexi and he wants to meet."

"Fuck."

"Yeah, fuck pretty much covers it."

Blaze relayed Bradley's call. "If you think for one minute you're going into this without backup, you're sorely mistaken."

"I get it, but we need to be smart about this."

"We will be, son. We will be. This son of a bitch is going down."

"If he..."

"Nope. We aren't thinking that way. She's smart. She's resourceful. She's resilient. You stay strong for her and she'll stay strong for you."

"Okay. Okay."

"Come on. Let's get back over to the station and make a plan of some kind. We'll pull Shaver in and see what we can come up with."

Blaze looked back and forth between the blood spot where Lucky had lain and the broken shards of glass and spots of blood where Lexi had gone down. "Yeah. Let's do this."

Chapter Eighteen

Lexi's head throbbed. She could feel the dried blood caked on her face and her vision was blurry. For a moment she had no idea where she was or what had happened. Then in a flash, it all came back to her in a blinding fury. Bradley was alive. He was alive and he'd taken her again. He'd shot and probably killed Lucky. He intended to kill Blaze. She'd never felt more helpless in her life than what she'd felt over the past week.

She'd always been proud of how strong and independent she'd become after losing her parents and Jackson, how resourceful. Now, she only felt failure.

Through squinted eyes, she looked around once more and realized she was in the town park. How ironic, she thought, that the place she'd just been discussing as the perfect spot for their wedding would likely be the place where one or both of them would die instead.

She was gagged again. This time a cloth stretched across her mouth and was tied tightly behind her head. Her wrists and feet were restrained as well and she lay on her side with her head on the grass looking across one of the paths that weaved its way through the park. After a brief moment of struggling, she managed to get herself off the ground and sitting up straight. Once she was up she looked around once more. Not only was her vision blurry, but she was seeing double. Great, she thought, I've got a concussion.

She had no idea where Bradley was but assumed he was nearby. He certainly wasn't going to go to all this trouble to then leave her on her own. There was a still-ness in the air that added to her wariness. She knew if she tried to escape he'd shoot her on the spot, not that she could move much anyway with the way he had her restrained. She closed her eyes against the bright sunshine, resigned to having to wait and see how every-thing played out in the end.

When the unmistakable sound of someone ap-proaching reached her ears, she raised her head. The image of the person approaching waved before her eyes, but she knew that form, knew that body intimately, and what tiny bit of hope she'd been hanging onto bloomed inside her heart.

There she was. Blaze wanted to run to her, to gather her in his arms, and never let go. It was what he wanted but he knew he had to wait.

Their plan was simple. They didn't have time to plan anything more elaborate. Blaze would approach the meeting spot taking a normal route through the park. And though he was told to come alone, everyone at the meeting had agreed – they were in this together. Sheriff Kaminski would approach from the back end of the park and Deputy Shaver would come in from the west, each of them taking a circuitous route to reach their destination, letting Blaze arrive first and staying out of sight until they were needed.

He stopped in the path approximately thirty yards from where she sat up against a tree waiting for him. He dared not get any closer, hoping to keep her out of any potential line of fire. He wondered where Bradley was. He wondered if she was okay. He wondered if he would ever escape his past and get to live out the future he wanted with the love of his life.

He didn't have to wait long to have his first question answered. Within a couple of minutes of him stopping on the path, Bradley stepped out from behind a tree opposite of the one Lexi leaned against, his gun aimed at Blaze.

"Let's get this over with."

"Don't be in such a hurry, Deputy." Disgust weaved its way through his voice and he practically spat out Blaze's title. "We're going to have a conversation. Then, well, then it's easy. I'm going to kill you." With a smirk on his face, he turned his gun on Lexi.

"I loved your brother as if he was my own. Hell, I was closer to him than my own brother. If I could have prevented it I would have."

"That's just it. You could have. You could have stopped it from happening. I read the reports. You left him. You chose to leave him when it was your job to be there for him, to protect him."

"It wasn't that simple and if you've read the reports then you know it wasn't that simple."

"Yeah, right."

"Do you think that a day, a moment even, has passed since Brandon died in my arms that I haven't carried some amount of guilt with me? That there haven't been times when the guilt almost drowned me with its presence? I wish it hadn't happened the way it did. I wish I could have saved him, too. I wish he was still here. I wish I could tell him so much more."

"You could have!"

"Maybe. Maybe I could have stopped it." Anguish tore through his voice. "Let me ask you something, could you have done it? Could you have let that little girl die?

She was a baby. A baby for God's sake! She deserved a chance to live!"

"So did Brandon!" Anger and frustration made him begin to pace as he spoke. "He deserved to live! He deserved to do everything that you've managed to do since you left the military. He deserved to find a woman, to build a home and a life. And you, you don't deserve any of it. Not after you let him die."

"Maybe I don't deserve happiness, but do you think he would be pleased with you? With what you've done? You're his brother, his twin. He told me all about you, about how close the two of you were. He was proud of you, of the person you became, of all you'd done with your life. Do you think he would be proud now? Do you think he would want you to handle things this way?"

"Stop! Stop! You took everything from me. My brother, the man I was going to spend my life with. Everything!"

At that moment Sheriff Kaminski made his appearance and Deputy Shaver did the same mere seconds later. Both of them had their guns drawn and aimed at Bradley who had immediately trained his own gun on Lexi who sat watching everything with fear clear and evident on her face.

"Drop your gun, Son."

"Not a chance old man. I knew you wouldn't come alone, Blaze. You don't have any idea how I knew, but

I knew." Suddenly he began to laugh. "Shit... You guys are so damn clueless. You have no idea what's going on right beneath your noses."

Blaze cut his eyes over to the Sheriff and then over to where Deputy Shaver stood. "Well, then, how about you fill us in? What are we missing?"

Once again he laughed, hysteria beginning to break through as he continued talking. "Hell, at this point, I'm fucked either way, so I may as well fill you in. The fire? You guys think that was me. It wasn't."

Blaze nodded his head in agreement. "Yeah. I had already figured that out. That belongs to whoever is running the drug ring around here."

"You're still not getting it. Don't you see? The drug ring? You know who it is. You know the person running it."

Blaze and Sheriff Kaminski looked toward each other and then back. Deputy Shaver shifted foot to foot and glanced at his co-workers before returning his attention to Bradley.

"Interesting." The Sheriff cocked his head to the side as he contemplated. "I'm curious. Are you going to fill us in or are you going to keep us guessing?"

"Oh, it's so much more fun to keep you guessing, but I'm certain it will all come to light very soon." With that statement, Bradley turned to Deputy Shaver and grinned, amusement alight in his eyes. "Won't it, Deputy?"

In the blink of an eye, Blaze drew his gun and aimed at his co-worker. "What's he talking about, Shaver?"

"I have no idea. He's insane." Once again he shifted and sweat began to roll down the side of his face.

Bradley began to laugh harder. "See? Do you get it now?"

Blaze nodded his head, "Yeah. Things are getting clearer by the moment."

With his gun still trained on Bradley, Sheriff Kaminski asked, "Why? Why are you doing it, Shaver?"

"You don't understand."

"No, no we don't. Enlighten us."

"It's supposed to be mine."

"What is?"

"I've worked at this job for years and during that time I've been overlooked repeatedly. I should have been named sheriff. Instead, they brought in an old, has been detective from New York City. I was mad, but I dealt with it. I told myself over and again to be patient, that one day I wouldn't be overlooked. I worked hard. I did everything asked of me and went over and above. And still, I waited."

Bradley continued to laugh, never once dropping his gun, keeping it aimed at Blaze while Lexi looked on in wide-eyed terror.

"Then," Shaver continued, "here comes Michael "Blaze" Blaisure, former military, former special ops, brilliant strategist, crack shot, and golden child. You took him under your wing like he's your long-lost son. It didn't take me long to realize your plans. When you finally leave you're going to appoint him as sheriff. Don't deny it. I've seen the way it was going to go for a long time now."

"And just how did peddling drugs in the community play into this?"

"Don't you see, Sheriff," Blaze broke in, "he was trying to set it up so he would get the collar. He's been working to make it look like he's the hometown hero. Who better to appoint as sheriff than the person who broke up the drug ring infecting our little community?"

"Yes. I see. You're right, Blaze, and that right there is just one more reason you should be appointed sheriff when I do finally walk away. Your brilliant mind is quick."

With that, Bradley spoke up, "Oops! I guess the cat is out of the bag now, Shaver!"

"Yeah. It is. And since it is, and I'm going down, I see no reason not to do this." With that, he fired, the sound of the shot echoed throughout the park and Bradley's body jerked with the impact. When it did, his hand tightened on his gun and pulled the trigger. As the second shot sounded ominously, his body fell lifelessly to the ground. He would no longer be a problem for Blaze and Lexi.

Blaze lowered his gun and was across the park in an instant tackling Deputy Shaver to the ground. They scuffled, arms swinging, fists punching, but not for long before Blaze punched him in the face and knocked him out. Once he was immobile, Blaze cuffed him and stood, taking a moment to catch his breath.

"Blaze! Get over here! Now!"

He looked to where Sheriff Kaminski had called from and to his horror it was the tree where Lexi had been sitting watching the interaction. With phone in hand, the sheriff looked at Blaze, worry and fear evident on his face. "I need an ambulance. GSW. Victim is a thirty-year-old female. GSW is to the chest and she's bleeding out.

Blaze's world was reduced to a pinpoint. Icy fear skated down his spine and spread like a vicious virus throughout his body. He ran and as he ran he stripped off his shirt to use as a compress on her wound.

"Oh, God! Lexi! Angel! No! Dear God, no!" He gathered her in his arms and pressed his shirt to the wound. Blood soon soaked through and onto his hands.

Once again sirens screeched through the sleepy little town of Durbin, West Virginia. And as they did, Blaze begged and pleaded with God or whoever might be listening. As the blood continued to pour from her body, past and present collided in his mind and tears began to stream down his face.

As he cradled her, he threw his head back and did the only other thing he could do.

He screamed his rage, his fear. He screamed his anguish and his pain. He screamed for her. He screamed for himself. He screamed for the past, the present, the future. He screamed for their hopes and dreams. He screamed until his voice went hoarse and even then he continued to scream.

In agony, he waited and hoped and prayed.

To be continued...

Acknowledgments

Dear reader: Thank you so much for letting me share this story with you. Yes, there is more to come. I will do my best to not leave you waiting and wondering any longer than I absolutely have to. I have quite a few people to thank, so please bear with me.

To my husband and children: You are my heart. I'm not always the easiest person to live with, yet somehow the three of you always love and support me – no matter what I throw at you. This past year has been extremely hard on us and I can't thank you enough for standing by me during my storms. There are more storm clouds on the horizon, but I know our rainbow is coming. I love you so much!

To Matthew: I say and will always say, it was kismet we met. You have helped me so much in the book world and even though you are chasing other dreams now, I know I can always count on you to point me in the right direction. You continue to inspire me in so many ways. Thank you for your encouragement and for always calling me on my shit. You know overthinking is my jam and I can't thank you enough for helping me turn my brain off! Thank you for checking on me during some of the hardest moments of my life. I'd be lost without you! This trilogy is 'Your Song.'

To Golden: Thank you for sharing your knowledge and expertise. You keep me on track, which is not an easy feat. I'm sure by now you know I tend to derail easily. Thank you for working with me to get my ducks in a row with all the publishing sites. Also, thank you for these kick-ass covers! You're amazing!

To Paula: I love you long time! You're my sister from another mister. The ego that brings balance to my id and superego. Thank you for always being there for me and providing direction when I most need it. Also, thank you for buying my books even though you can't read them. (I promise it isn't me in the sex scenes!)

To Kim and Beth: I don't know what I'd do without both of you and our girls nights! Maybe we don't close the bars down as often or in quite the same way as we used to, but we do still make it happen! Thank you both for listening to my outrageous stories, for sharing your own outrageous stories, and for adding color to my existence. Having you both in my life and knowing I can (and have) talked to you about any and everything is priceless! I love you guys!

To my Sexy Beach Mamas – Julie, Megan, Staci, Brenda, and Jen: I'm ready for any "of death" drink y'all want to throw my way. Gym. Beach. Drink. (Maybe a side of drunk mini golf!) Thank you all for loving me and for all our drunken memories!

To Dwayne: You've been there for me since day one – unconditionally. Thank you for always being a shoulder I can cry on. Thank you for always making me laugh. Thank you for loving my crazy ass no matter what idiocy pours from my mouth. Our saying may be "It is what it is," but your friendship makes "it" much more bearable!

To Jill, Loren & Kalyani: Some of our greatest blessings come from untenable situations. It wasn't always easy making that drive to the warehouse every day for a year and a half, but getting to know you guys made it worthwhile. You guys can stalk me anytime you want!

More By Dawn Love

Meet the Cassidy Brothers! These sexy, single brothers may not be looking for their happily ever after, but fate has other ideas. Join Cade, Cameron, Colton, Calvin, and Colby as their destinies are revealed!

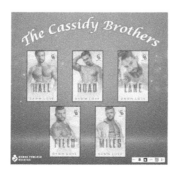

He fell in love when he was eight years old. His summer vacation had led to a childhood crush that he'd never forgotten. Though he didn't realize it, he'd looked for her in every woman he'd dated. She'd fallen in love, too. The lonely little girl she'd been had found a new friend, making for her best vacation ever. She's all grown up now but still lonely, perhaps more so than ever. A walk on the beach will change both their worlds forever.

She fled the city searching for a new life. Leaving all she'd ever known behind her had been a snap decision, but if things go her way, it will be the best decision she will have ever made. He was looking for love without even realizing it. When she walked into his bar seeking a job, he had no idea she would be the love he was waiting for. They can only have their happy ending if her disastrous past doesn't track her down and destroy the life they want to build together.

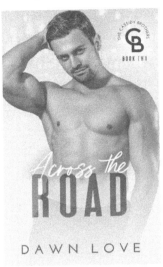

He's the bad boy of the family who hides his heart of gold behind a tough exterior, a leather jacket, and a Harley. He works hard and plays harder. He's known for his wild and wicked ways, but all he really wants is love. She is only in town for the summer and plans to make the most of it. She's had her future laid out for as long as she can remember, and if her plans come together, she'll make a huge leap toward fulfilling her dreams. Their chance meeting causes sparks to fly and desires to soar.

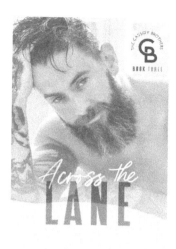

DAWN LOVE

Calvin has dreamed of playing in the big leagues his entire life. He works hard, trains hard, and plays harder. Having watched his older brothers falling in love and starting families, he determines that he just isn't about that kind of life. Being free to play the field romantically and sexually, while he plays the field for a living, is what it's all about in his book. Jillian has loved sports for as long as she can remember and the camera loves Jillian. She's smart, quick, and witty - everything a major sports broadcast needs to keep the fans interested and on their toes. She loves being single and has no intentions of settling down any time soon. It only takes one night for their carefully laid plans to get hit out of the park.

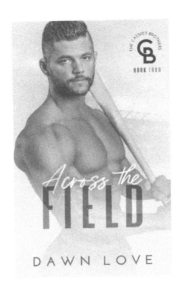

Colby Cassidy is a player. He's always been a player and feels no need to change his wicked ways. The women he gets involved with know the score and endgame. He's always excelled at whatever he's done and his sexual exploits are no different. Over the past few years he's watched his brothers fall, one by one, head over heels into the bliss of love and happily ever after. Being last-man-standing has him constantly looking over his shoulder and worrying that it's only a matter of time before he finds himself on the ledge. Will he jump, fall, or be pushed into what he never knew he wanted? Juliette Tate's life belongs to the stage. Years and years of ballet has trained her body hard for the rigors of the dance world and she's finally started to make a name for herself in the Big Apple. When she suddenly finds herself in a tight spot, she does what she has to do to scrape by. She never thought her dance skills would be used quite the way they are, but she's making the most of it. At least she is until her secret is discovered and the one man she has a hard time saying no to, steps in with an indecent proposal. Will fate tear them apart or push them together?

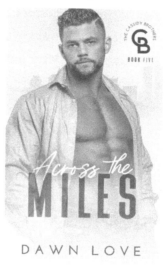

Looking for romantic suspense? Dive into the Mountain Mayhem series and meet Blaze and Lexi!

They say when life hands you lemons, make lemon-ade.

But for Lexi Lane, life didn't hand her those lemons. Instead, they were hurled from a grenade launcher.

It's been almost five years since her world detonated around her, and she's moved on from that sour time in her life - or so she thinks. Hiding out in the mountains of West Virginia has given her the solitude she's needed to survive, but surviving is all she's done. When a stranger crashes into her life, will she finally be able to open herself to feel again? To love again?

Michael "Blaze" Blaisure has devoted his life to righting some of the wrongs in the world. Part of a covert military unit, he has traveled from country to country and seen the pits of hell first-hand. After witnessing more death and despair than his heart and soul could take, he makes the decision to change directions and choose a new path. But will that path lead to acceptance and forgiveness for his part in tragedy and death? All it takes is a mountain, a storm, and the hand of fate to open their eyes to new horizons. But when danger appears, will it separate them, or bring them closer than ever?

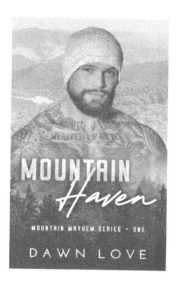

Welcome to Canyon Creek!

Falling in love with your best friend's sister may not be taboo to everyone.

For Logan Grant, it's simply unthinkable. A man of his word, Logan would never break a pact he made, no matter how much heart-wrenching agony he suffers each time he thinks of the woman of his dreams. Sera was, is, and always will be the one who owns him – heart, mind, body, and soul. Staying true to his word is becoming harder and harder the more time they spend together. As the sexual tension between them grows, so does his need to be with her.

A best-selling author, Seraphina Matthias has decided to take her research to the next level, and she knows there's only one man she wants to fill the role of muse and partner in discovery. Close friends, Logan has always been there to catch her as she stumbles through life. Although she's never really thought about him sexually or romantically, she knows she trusts nobody else to help her with her research – even if he is completely unaware of her intentions.

Will Logan be able to stay true to himself and honor his agreement while his heart's desire begins to play a wicked game? Will Sera's secrets cause her to lose his trust and friendship? His love?

About Author

Dawn Love was born in Mayfield, Kentucky, and spent the first twenty-six years of her life there. Always a creative person and an avid reader, she began writing stories for her own entertainment as a teen, and her love of writing continued to grow into adulthood. Meeting the love of her life brought many changes, including moving 900 miles away from home and settling on the

Delmarva Peninsula where she resides on her 50-acre farm. Now the mother of two teenagers, she spends her free time creating the characters and stories of her fantasies. She also writes an internationally read Blog where she gives her readers a glimpse into the craziness of her day-to-day life, her mind, and all that the world throws her way.